FANNY PACKS AND FOUL PLAY

by

Dorothy Howell

ISBN: 978-0-9856930-4-6

Published in the United States of America

Fanny Packs and Foul Play

DEDICATION:

With love to Stacy, Judy, Seth and Brian

I couldn't have written this novella without the support of a lot of people. Some of them are: Stacy Howell, Judith Branstetter, David Howell, Martha Cooper, Evie Cook, Webcrafters Design, and William F. Wu, Ph.D.

Special thanks to the readers and friends who contributed the lawyer jokes: Carol Beyner, Gina Cresse, Joyce Meyer, Marilynn Stella, and all the others who wished to remain anonymous.

Books by Dorothy Howell

The Haley Randolph Mystery Series
Handbags and Homicide
Purses and Poison
Shoulder Bags and Shootings
Clutches and Curses
Slay Bells and Satchels
Tote Bags and Toe Tags
Evening Bags and Executions
Duffel Bags and Drownings
Beach Bags and Burglaries
Fanny Packs and Foul Play

The Dana Mackenzie Mystery Series

Fatal Debt
Fatal Luck

FANNY PACKS AND FOUL PLAY

By

Dorothy Howell

Chapter 1

"I'd die for a new handbag," Marcie said.

I was ready to kill for one but didn't say so. Marcie had been my best friend since forever. She already knew.

We were at the Galleria in Sherman Oaks, one of L.A.s many upscale areas, scoping out the shops and boutiques. Marcie and I shared a love—okay, it was really an obsession, but so what—of designer handbags   .

All things fashion-forward were of supreme interest to us. But that was to be expected. We were both in our mid-twenties, smack in the middle of our we-have-to-look-great-now-before-it's-too-late years. Marcie was a petite blonde, and I, Haley Randolph, was tall with dark hair. Marcie was sensible and level headed, and I—well, I wasn't. But that's not the point. We're still BFFs and that's what matters.

Since we'd exhausted all the places we should have been able to find a terrific handbag, we moved through the open-air shopping center past the stores, restaurants, and office spaces toward the parking garage. I had on a fabulous black business suit, since I was on my lunch hour, and Marcie had taken the day off from her job at a bank downtown so she had on jeans, a sweater, and a blazer. We looked great—perfect for a November afternoon.

"What the heck is wrong with all the designers?" I asked, as we passed one of the boutiques we'd already checked out. "All they have to do is design handbags.

That's it. And I haven't seen one decent bag in months."

"It hasn't been months," Marcie pointed out. "Only a few weeks."

She was right, of course. Marcie was almost always right.

I was in no mood.

"You've been kind of crabby lately," Marcie said, as only a BFF can. "What's wrong?"

"Nothing," I insisted.

Marcie gave me a we're-best-friends look which was usually comforting, but not today. My life had been a roller coaster for a while now, but I'd been doing okay with it. I had a great job as an event planner at L.A. Affairs and … and …and—wait. Hang on. Was that the only good thing I had going?

Oh my God. It was.

I still had my will-this-nightmare-ever-end part-time sales clerk job at the how-the-heck-does-this-crappy-place-stay-in-business Holt's Department Store. My mom was driving me crazy—no, really, crazier than usual—over prep for her upcoming Thanksgiving dinner that I was expected to attend. I'd broken up with my hot, handsome, fabulous official boyfriend Ty Cameron. I was staring down the barrel of the single girl's Bermuda Triangle of holidays—Christmas, New Years, and Valentine's Day— and lately it seemed that if civilization were dying, men would rather let it go than date me.

So was it too much to ask that a designer somewhere come up with a fabulous new handbag that would soothe my worries, boost my spirits, and keep me going until things turned around?

Apparently, it was.

"If you want to talk, I'll be home late tonight," Marcie

said. "I'm having dinner with Beau."

Oh, yeah, and Marcie had a new boyfriend—which I'm really happy about. Really.

"Have fun," I said, which I totally meant.

Marcie had kissed her share of frogs, and while Beau might not be her prince, he was at least a really nice guy, good looking with a great job, and liked to go places and do things with her—which was why I was really happy for her. Really.

We waved good-bye and Marcie continued on toward the parking garage. I headed the other way through the Galleria and crossed the busy Sepulveda and Ventura intersection to the building that housed L.A. Affairs, an event planning company to the stars—and everyone else who mattered in Hollywood and Los Angeles. It was my job to execute fabulous parties for people who had more money than they knew what to do with so they spent it on extravagant, outrageous, mine-is-better-than-yours events, then left it up to me to, somehow, pull it off.

I took the elevator up to the L.A. Affairs office on the third floor and walked inside. A florist on our approved list—who wanted us to keep booking them for events—had decorated the lobby with pumpkins, corn stalks, and mum plants.

Mindy, our receptionist, was at her post. She was somewhere in her forties, with a waistline that attested to her total commitment to the Food Network, and blonde hair she's sprayed into the shape of a mushroom.

If it's true that we learn from our mistakes, Mindy will soon be a genius.

"Are you ready to party?" Mindy exclaimed.

She's supposed to chant that ridiculous slogan to clients, yet for some unknown reason I was continually

—

5

bombarded with it.

"I work here," I told her, for about the zillionth time. "Okay? I'm an employee. Here. You don't have to keep saying that to me."

Mindy made a pouty face and shook her head. "Oh, dear, someone is having a bad day."

I walked away.

Just past the cube farm and the client interview rooms I turned down the hallway where the offices, supply room, conference rooms, and breakroom were located. I desperately needed to hit the snack cabinet. I was long overdue for a chocolate fix, and the mocha frappuccino—the most fabulous drink in the world—that I'd gotten after lunch at Starbucks—the most fabulous place in the world—had worn off.

I ducked into my private office—a great space with neutral furniture and splashes of blue and yellow, and a huge window with a view of the Galleria—and was about to drop my handbag into my desk drawer when my cell phone rang. It was Mom.

Oh crap.

"Good news," she announced when I answered.

Mom's news was seldom good—for me, anyway.

"I've figured out how to remedy my seating chart problem," she said

Mom said it as if she'd just hammered out a peace treaty in the Middle East, and while she did wish for world peace—she was, after all, a former beauty queen—I'm not sure she was even aware there were problems in that region of the world.

Really, how could she know if it wasn't covered in *Vogue*?

"Oh?" I murmured, as I dropped into my desk chair.

"I've been quite concerned about your sister lately," Mom said.

To the untrained observer, it appeared that Mom's seating chart and her concerns for my sister weren't related. I knew the connection would be revealed—as long as I was patient enough to wait.

I'm not usually that patient.

"She hasn't been herself since she broke up with Lars," Mom said.

I had no idea who Lars was.

My sister was a little younger than me. She attended UCLA, did some modeling, and was a near perfect genetic copy of our mother.

I wasn't.

"So," Mom said, "I'm going to find a dinner companion for your sister on Thanksgiving."

I lurched forward in my chair. She was going to— what?

"That way she won't be lonely and sad," Mom said.

She was going to set up my sister with a blind date?

"Someone from a good family, of course," Mom said. "Young and handsome, well educated."

What about me? She knew I'd broken up with Ty.

"Which will also solve my seating chart problem," Mom said.

No way did I want my mother to set me up with somebody—but that's not the point.

"I'm calling around now to see who's eligible," Mom said. "I'll let you know."

She hung up. I jabbed the red button on my cell phone and tossed it into my handbag.

Oh my God, I couldn't believe this. My life was locked in a death spiral and *this* was what Mom wanted to do?

The office phone on my desk rang. It was Mindy.

"Hello? Hello? Haley?" she asked, when I picked up.

I drew a quick breath, trying to calm myself.

"Yes, Mindy?"

"Oh, yes, hello. I'd like to speak to Haley," Mindy said.

Good grief.

"I'm Haley," I said.

"Oh, jiminy, so you are," Mindy said and giggled. "So, anyway, there's a Mr. Douglas in the office—no, he's on the phone. Yes, he's on the phone, holding. He wants to come by and see you right now."

A man wanted an appointment? In person? Immediately?

That could only mean one thing—he wanted to plan a surprise party for his wife or girlfriend. Somebody he desperately loved, thought the world of, wanted to impress and flatter, and shower with special moments.

No way.

"Tell him to forget it," I barked, and hung up.

Two people had told me today that I was in a crappy mood. Well, screw them.

I grabbed my handbag and an event portfolio and left.

Chapter 2

As holidays went, Thanksgiving was definitely the easiest—and believe me, I know.

After months of meticulous planning and serious hand-holding with neurotic hostesses over dozens of this-one-could-send-me-screaming-from-the-building events, I was ready for something as simple as orchestrating Thanksgiving dinner for my clients. This would be the calm before the Christmas season when everyone was stressed-out, overwhelmed, and exhausted by attempting yet another this-year-it-will-be-perfect holiday.

I mean, really, what special occasion could be easier than Thanksgiving? You didn't have to squeeze into a formal dress, cook over a hot smoky barbecue grill, risk a sunburn, strain your neck looking up at fireworks, spend a fortune, do major shopping, or make yourself crazy over what gifts to buy or—yikes!—what gifts you might get. There was no fighting the crowds at the mall, the beach, or the ballpark. All you had to do was put up with your relatives for a few hours and eat—a full bar helped, too, of course.

The afternoon sun shone bright and clear in the cloudless sky as I drove on the 101 toward the home of Veronica and Patrick Spencer-Taft, my this-one-will-be-the-easiest clients. They lived in Calabasas, an affluent city of multi-million dollar mansions situated in the hills west of the San Fernando Valley where celebrities, pop icons, actors, athletes, musicians, and reality TV stars lived.

Veronica and Patrick weren't any of those things. They were a young couple who were super in love—and I'm really happy for them. Really.

Veronica had come to the L.A. Affairs office several weeks ago for help with a Thanksgiving Day feast she and Patrick wanted to throw for their employees to thank them for their hard work. I'd liked her right away. She was about my age, a petite blue-eyed blonde transplant from Arkansas, Alabama, Amarillo—I don't know, one of the A places—who radiated what-the-heck-let's-do-it excitement about everything.

Veronica and Patrick had started Pammy Candy a year or so ago and it had skyrocketed, enabling them to move out of their Culver City newlywed's bungalow and buy a huge place in one of the most trendy locations in the Los Angeles area.

Patrick didn't need the candy business income. He was from an old money family—as demonstrated by his hyphenated last name—that had settled here generations ago and helped found Los Angeles.

Veronica, however, was a different story—a way different story.

I exited the freeway and wound through the hills to the street where Veronica and Patrick were making their new home. It was gorgeous—and I'm really happy for them. Really.

They'd purchased the property a couple of months ago and were splitting their time between here and their Culver City bungalow while major renovations were underway. The construction guys were working overtime, trying to get everything finished in time for the Thanksgiving feast.

I eased up behind a plumbing company van stopped at the neighborhood's security gate and waited until the guard let it through. I pulled forward and showed the guard my driver's license. Even though I'd been here numerous times, he still looked closely at my picture and checked his list of approved visitors before opening the gate.

"Enjoy your visit, Miss Randolph," he said.

"Thanks," I called, and drove through.

I caught up with the van a few moments later. The neighborhood streets rambled through the canyons and hills, all heavily landscaped to keep out any stalker, paparazzi, or tourist who might somehow slip in.

At the Spencer-Taft house—really, it was a mansion— the plumbing van pulled around back. I parked my Honda in the circular driveway alongside a Mazda. A white convertible BMW, a black Bentley, and a silver Mercedes were nearby.

I'd been here several times to discuss the Thanksgiving feast with Veronica. She was super busy working at Pammy Candy with Patrick and overseeing the renovations at the house, so I'd met with her here to accommodate her schedule—plus it was a good excuse for me to get out of the office.

The house had a Mediterranean vibe with eight bedrooms, ten bathrooms, a media room, a game room, a fabulous kitchen, and servants' quarters, among other extravagances. Out back were a patio, pool, and spa set among lush landscaping, an organic garden, a koi pond, and a breathtaking view of the canyons and mountains.

I grabbed the L.A. Affairs event portfolio and reached for my handbag, a Burberry satchel. The bag had seemed the perfect complement to my business suit when I'd selected it this morning, but now I wasn't feeling so great about it.

Yeah, okay, it was a terrific purse, and it had been a major must-have when I'd bought it. But, jeez, that was a long time ago—two, maybe three weeks. Time had moved on and I desperately needed something new. Marcie hadn't seemed all that troubled about this major glitch in my life today at lunch, which I didn't get—I'm mean, come on, it wasn't like I'd just lost my first baby tooth.

Obviously, I was going to have to ramp up my efforts to find a new, totally awesome handbag.

There was a lot of commotion at the front of the house as I got out of my Honda. Landscapers were digging trenches, laying new irrigation pipe, weeding the flower beds, and cutting back overgrown plants. Scaffolding had been erected near the massive double front doors and three electricians were installing light fixtures. Workmen were unloading pallets of decorative stone from a delivery truck.

The job foreman stood with two women, holding an iPad, pointing and explaining something. Veronica wasn't with them, which didn't surprise me.

One of the women was Patrick's mother, Julia Spencer-Taft.

I didn't actually hate her—yet, anyway—but she was pushing me in that direction big-time.

Julia was mid-fifties, tall with perfectly coiffed dark hair, and displayed understated elegance and exquisite taste in her ultra-expensive clothing. She carried herself with a regal I've-been-better-than-you-for-generations way that was, I'm sure, engrained in her DNA.

Standing beside her was Erika, the decorator who was masterminding the changes to the interior of the house. I didn't especially like her, either, though I wasn't sure why.

She was around my age, tall, blonde, and gorgeous—which I guess was reason enough.

I'd crossed paths with the oh-so-charming Julia Spencer-Taft a few times since planning began for the Thanksgiving event. She didn't know me personally but she was aware of L.A. Affairs' reputation so she had to at least act as if she liked me. Erika had been pleasant—after she checked out the Louis Vuitton satchel I'd had with me that first day and decided, I suppose, that I was good enough for her to speak with.

But now it was go-time. I had to put aside my dislike for Julia and Erika and see to it that Veronica and Patrick put on a Thanksgiving feast that would wow their employees. This didn't suit me, of course, but there it was—and it had nothing to do with the fact that two people had said I was in a crabby mood today.

"No, no, that simply won't do," Julia said to the foreman as I walked up. She huffed irritably. "It is the absolute height of bad taste."

Erika drew back from the iPad as if she'd smelled something stinky and then exchanged a knowing look with Julia.

"Horrid beyond words," she agreed.

Julia held up a carefully manicured hand and the foreman had the good sense to move the iPad away from her.

"Completely unacceptable," Julia decreed.

"I discussed this with Veronica," the foreman said. "She liked the design and wanted to—"

Julia drew herself up and averted her eyes, indicating she had no intention of gazing upon so hideous a sight any longer or listening to his explanation—especially if it involved Veronica.

He stepped back and said, "I'll have another design ready for you later today."

She didn't acknowledge him as he walked away, which I'm sure he was grateful for.

"Hello," I said, using my I-get-paid-to-be-nice-to-snooty-people-like-you voice.

They gave me the standard you're-the-hired-help greeting.

"Where's Veronica?" I asked. No way did I want to involve either of them with the Thanksgiving feast planning, if I didn't have to.

"Inside," Julia told me and pursed her lips, "probably envisioning mauve carpeting and brass bath fixtures."

Erika snickered.

Yeah, I was on the verge of clicking these two onto my mental I-hate-you list.

The front door opened and Andrea, Veronica's personal assistant, walked out carrying the tools of her trade, an iPad and a cell phone.

"Hi, Haley," she said, as she joined us.

Andrea was about my age, short with dark hair. She managed to look both fashion-forward and competent at the same time—not easy to pull off.

"Veronica is in the master suite," she said, and nodded toward the house. "She should be down any minute. Today's the big day."

I remembered then that some of Veronica's relatives from back east were scheduled to arrive this afternoon for a visit. She'd been super excited about having her own family close by, for a change.

And, really, who could blame her?

Andrea glanced at her wristwatch. "They should arrive shortly."

14

Julia uttered a barely audible grunt and shared another knowing look with Erika.

"It seems the Thanksgiving plans are shaping up great," Andrea said, with more enthusiasm than was necessary.

"Veronica does appear to enjoy a good meal," Julia commented, causing Erika to put on a very poor attempt at suppressing a smile.

"Oh, here they come," Andrea said.

Everyone turned as a black limousine approached, then pulled into the circular driveway. The doors opened and three women and a teenage girl piled out.

Erika gasped.

"Oh, for God's sake," Julia muttered.

"I'll call Veronica," Andrea said, and put her cell phone to her ear.

The four guests were in high spirits, smiling, chatting, and directing the chauffeur as he unloaded their luggage.

"I've never seen so much traffic in all my born days," one of the women declared.

"And expensive cars everywhere you look," another exclaimed.

"Can you believe this weather?" the third one said, giving herself a little shake.

I figured all of the women for somewhere on the high side of fifty. Two of them had on stretch pants and T-shirts, and the other wore a lavender track suit. They all had fanny packs belted around their waists. None of them wore makeup. Their hair was I'm-over-forty short.

The teenager had on jeans, sneakers, and a sweatshirt. Her blonde hair was in a loose ponytail and she had earbuds plugged into her ears which, it seemed, was a universal accessory for someone her age, fourteen or fifteen, I guessed.

"Welcome," Andrea said, joining them.

They turned and gasped as they looked up at the house.

"Oh my Lord, would you look at this place," one of them said.

"It's just like one of those mansions on TV," another said.

"Maybe we can film one of those reality shows here," the woman in the track suit said.

They all laughed. The teenager girl ignored them; she seemed more interested in the construction guys.

"I'm Andrea, Veronica's assistant," Andrea said.

"Did you hear that?" one of the women asked, nudging the other two. "Our little Veronica has her own assistant."

"We're just proud as punch of her," another of them added.

Andrea gestured toward the house and said, "Veronica is upstairs. She'll be down in a second."

"Can't wait a second—long ride," the woman in the track suit declared, then darted past Andrea into the house.

Andrea, who had studied photos of her employer's guests—standard procedure for a top tier P.A.—introduced everyone.

"May I present Veronica's aunts Melanie and Cassie? Her aunt Renée just went inside. And this is Melanie's daughter, Brandie," she said, drawing me into their circle. "This is Haley Randolph. She's the event planner for the Thanksgiving Day dinner."

"It's so nice to meet you," I said, and really it was. The women were thoroughly enjoying themselves, completely thrilled by the new sights they were experiencing. The teenage girl looked embarrassed, as a teenager would.

"An event planner?" Melanie gasped.

"That must be more fun than a Friday afternoon off," Cassie declared.

I couldn't help smiling. Yeah, I liked these gals.

I expected the introductions to continue but when I glanced around, I realized that Julia and Erika had disappeared. Andrea did, too, then recovered by motioning the guests toward the front door.

"Please come inside," she said, and they headed into the house.

Andrea hung back and whispered, "I can't imagine what's delaying Veronica. She's been so excited about their arrival."

"Where's Patrick?" I asked.

"At the factory," she said. "He'll be here later."

"I'll check on Veronica," I offered, since it would be extremely bad form for Andrea to abandon the guests.

"Great, thanks," Andrea said. "The master suite is in the east wing. Turn right at the top of the stairs."

I followed everyone into the entryway. Even though I'd been here before I was still awed by the place. The vaulted ceiling soared past the second story and a massive staircase swept down to the marble floor. There were exquisite chandeliers and statuary niches. Huge rooms opened up in all directions, some of them furnished and decorated, others occupied by workmen who were laying carpet and painting. The whole thing could have come off looking like a don't-touch-anything museum, but the warm colors and softened design features made it welcoming.

"Would you just look at this place?" Melanie murmured, craning her neck to take in everything.

"It's beautiful," Cassie agreed, shaking her head in wonder.

Brandie broke tradition with teenagers everywhere by staring wide-eyed and slack-jawed.

"I've got an emergency," Renée declared as she scampered into the entryway from one of the other rooms. "I've been all over this house and I can't find a bathroom."

"Oh, you and your old bladder," Melanie declared. "We can't take you anywhere."

"You can take me anywhere," Renée told her, "as long as there's a bathroom close by."

"This way," Andrea said, gesturing to a hall on the left.

She threw me a please-hurry look. I headed up the staircase as she herded everyone out of the entryway.

When I reached the second floor I heard hammering and a drill running somewhere off to my left where I figured the guest bedrooms were located. I turned right. At the end of a short hallway, double doors stood open so I walked inside.

The master suite was absolutely huge, with a retreat, a spacious bathroom, and four walk-in closets that I could readily spot. It was decorated in varying shades of blue, giving it a welcoming, restful vibe. Glass sliders led out to a balcony that overlooked the east side of the property and the wooded area that provided privacy.

"Veronica?" I called.

She didn't answer.

Okay, that was weird.

I knew how excited she was to have her family visit. She'd talked about it for weeks every time I'd consulted with her on the plans for the Thanksgiving feast. None of her relatives had been to Los Angeles before and she was anxious to show off her new home, the candy business, and her new life.

"Veronica?" I called again. "Your family is here."

I checked out the bathroom, the retreat, even the closets, but didn't see her. Huh. That was really weird. All I could figure was that she'd gone downstairs and I'd missed her.

As I headed for the door, I heard voices coming from the balcony. I crossed the bedroom and slipped through the glass sliders, expecting to see Veronica there talking with one of the servants or perhaps a workman.

Nobody was out there.

Voices floated up from below. I walked to the edge of the balcony and looked down. Three workmen were standing near the rose garden gesturing wildly and talking in urgent tones.

I realized why.

Veronica lay face down on the flagstone patio. A massive pool of blood oozed out around her. Two of the workers spotted me and started shouting. I couldn't understand them, but I didn't have to.

I already knew Veronica was dead.

Chapter 3

"I can't believe this happened," Andrea whispered. "It's just ... well, it's just freaky."

We were in a small den on the west side of the house, a comfortable room with plush furniture, a huge flat-screen, and windows that allowed in lots of sunlight and a view of the koi pond. Veronica's three aunts were huddled together on the sofa looking like trees in a petrified forest, staring straight ahead at nothing. Brandie was seated in a nearby chair fiddling with her cell phone. Servants had brought trays of sandwiches and drinks but nobody had touched anything.

The police and forensic techs were outside going about their business. We'd been asked to wait in here until we could give our statements. Patrick had arrived and was somewhere in the house, presumably with his mother; Andrea had mentioned that the rest of the family was out of the country. I had no idea where Erika was.

"Veronica must have been out on that balcony hundreds of times," Andrea said in a low voice. "What could have caused her to fall?"

I'd asked the workmen on the ground that same question, after I'd gotten over my initial shock. They'd all shaken their heads and told me they'd seen Veronica falling, but hadn't witnessed her actually going over the railing.

"Nobody seems to know. Maybe the police will find a

witness," I whispered back. "Were there any surveillance cameras on the property?"

Andrea shook her head. "Only by the front door. Veronica didn't like the idea of security cameras capturing their private lives."

Renée rose from the sofa, unzipped the jacket of her track suit and tossed it on a chair where everyone had dumped their belongings. She picked up one of the fanny packs I'd seen on all the gals when they'd arrived, and held it by the strap. It was orange, with a bedazzled turkey appliqué on the front.

"This whole trip has turned into nothing but a waste of time," she grumbled.

"How can you even think of something like that at a time like this?" Melanie demanded.

Brandie's gaze darted between her mother and her aunt.

"I can think whatever I want. And it's a perfectly valid comment," Renée said, shaking the fanny pack at her. "What are we supposed to do out here now? Look what Veronica's gone and done to us again."

Melanie shot to her feet. "It was an accident! A horrible accident!"

"I know it was an accident!" Renée said. "I didn't say it wasn't!"

"You'd better watch your mouth," Melanie told her.

"Stop it! Both of you!" Cassie rose and stepped between them. "This isn't the time or the place. Now, cut it out."

Obviously, these three aunts of Veronica's were sisters, and these were the roles they'd played for decades.

Renée and Melanie eyed each other for a few seconds, then Renée headed for the door.

"I need a smoke," she said.

"The police said we're not supposed to leave the room," Cassie called.

Renée ignored her and left, slamming the door behind her.

Melanie uttered a disgusted grunt and sat down, as did Cassie. Brandie folded her legs under her and burrowed deeper into the chair, and started punching buttons on her cell phone again.

Andrea and I exchanged an uncomfortable look, then she whispered, "I need to make a call."

"Me, too," I said.

I didn't, but I wanted out of that room. I figured Andrea felt the same.

Andrea held up her cell phone to the guests and said, "I'll be back in a couple of minutes."

I followed her out of the room without an explanation.

The house was silent as we walked down the hall to the entryway. Work had ceased, so there was no more equipment running. I figured all the construction guys had been rounded up and were being questioned. The lab techs were on the east side of the house, well out of view and earshot, thankfully.

"This whole thing is so sad," Andrea said, shaking her head. "I don't know how Patrick will ever get over losing her."

I'd seen the two of them together several times during the planning of their event and couldn't disagree.

"They seemed happy together," I said.

"It was love at first sight," Andrea said with a dreamy smile that made me think Veronica had shared the story with her more than once. "Patrick had gone back east to check on his family's holdings and he met Veronica selling candy at a farmers market. She said they both knew instantly that they were meant to be together forever. A fairytale match—the big city millionaire and the small town girl."

I smiled at the image that bloomed in my head, and said, "So that's how they started Pammy Candy?"

"Veronica was making and selling the candy at local swap meets, fairs, that sort of thing. Nothing big, just something for a little extra income," Andrea said. "Patrick saw the potential and wanted to take it national. Veronica always said their love grew along with the candy business. They eloped, sort of, and got married by candlelight in the small, rustic church Veronica had attended all her life. Just the two of them. Very romantic."

The image of my mom flashed in my head—and there was nothing romantic about it. If I, or my sister or brother, eloped robbing her of the opportunity to plan and attend our wedding, she would have a meltdown on a biblical scale.

"Patrick wanted to move the business to L.A. because he had more contacts here," Andrea said.

"Pammy Candy is everywhere now," I said. "It was a good decision."

Andrea's smile faded. "I'm not so sure. Veronica acted like everything was great, but it wasn't an easy adjustment for her. That's why Patrick hired me to help her."

Julia zinged into my head. I wondered how much she'd tried to smooth Veronica's transition.

Andrea glanced down the hallway. "I'd better get back in there. Coming?"

With so much gloom and doom in the room, I didn't really want to go in there again—which was bad of me, I know—but since I couldn't leave until the police had taken my statement and no way did I want to wander the grounds or the house and possibly run into Patrick or the lab guys, I followed Andrea back down the hallway.

Maybe I could get the staff to send in something chocolate—or a few beers.

Renée had returned from her smoke break when Andrea and I walked inside. Brandie was still pecking on her phone while Melanie and Cassie sat staring at nothing. Nobody spoke.

Jeez, I wish those police would hurry up so I could get out of here.

I mean that in the nicest way, of course.

No way could I take this much longer. I'd been here for hours and I had tons of work to do back at the office— okay, I didn't have that much to do but that's not the point.

Just as I was about to tell Andrea that I felt I was coming down with a touch of the stomach flu—my all-time favorite excuse to get out of most anything—the door opened. I expected to see detectives walk in but—oh my God, it was Jack Bishop.

Jack was a totally hot private detective. He was a little older than me, tall with dark hair and gorgeous eyes. We'd met a year or so ago when I'd been in the accounts payable department of a law firm at which Jack did consulting work—long story. We were kind-of-sort-of friends and colleagues because we'd helped each other out with cases from time to time.

There was a crazy heat between us that neither of us had acted on because, up until recently, I'd had an official boyfriend, Ty Cameron. Now, Jack and I were—well, I don't know what the heck we were.

Jack's entry into the room stirred the aunts. They

turned, did a double-take, and stared. Renée eased her shoulders back and sat up straighter on the sofa. Brandie yanked the clip from her ponytail and let her hair fall around her shoulders. Even Andrea stared—not that I blamed them, of course.

Jack nodded to everyone in the room, and sidled up next to me.

"I figured you'd be in here," he said in a low voice.

Thank God he didn't use his Barry White voice. I'm totally helpless against his Barry White voice.

"How did you know I was even in the house?" I asked.

Jack gave me his don't-question-the-master grin—which was way hot—then I realized that he'd recognized my Honda parked out front.

Good to know my deductive reasoning skills weren't completely destroyed in the presence of such a hot guy.

Jack cupped my elbow and walked me to the corner of the room.

"What are you doing here?" I asked quietly.

"Security," Jack said. "Pike Warner called me in."

Pike Warner was the law firm where I'd met Jack—and where I'd probably still be working if it hadn't been for that whole administrative-leave- investigation-pending thing—which represented the wealthiest, most prestigious clients in Los Angeles. I figured Julia had called them immediately upon learning of Veronica's death.

Families like the Spencer-Tafts didn't sign up for a gym membership without their attorneys at their elbow.

"What's happening?" I asked.

Jack angled his body so his back was to everyone else in the room—I'm sure they were all staring, and who could blame them—and leaned down.

"The cops are investigating the scene," he said, "very

thoroughly."

I figured they would. No way would they want to be responsible for a foul-up involving the death of a member of such a prominent family.

Then something else hit me.

"It was an accident, wasn't it?" I asked.

Jack shrugged. "We'll see."

A really ugly picture started to form in my head, but I pushed it out.

"Let me know if you hear anything," I said.

He nodded but didn't ask me to do the same—he already knew I would.

Maybe my relationship with Jack had lost some of its mystery.

Jack left the room, taking most of the heat with him, and I could see that everyone was getting restless and Renée was winding up for another smoke break. I was feeling antsy myself and was ready to break out my touch-of-the-stomach-flu excuse when the door opened and Julia walked in.

The vibe in the room amped up as everyone rose and crowded around her, expecting to, at long last, hear some definitive news. The aunts looked slightly more haggard than when they'd arrived, worn down by the sudden and unexpected loss of a loved one.

Julia appeared composed and in control, head up, shoulders back, facing the inevitable with the same we'll-go-on-no-matter-what spirit that the many generations of ancestors before her must have displayed.

She pressed her palms together and drew a breath.

"I'm so very sorry for your loss," she said, looking at each of Veronica's relatives in turn. "I know this is a blow none of you expected. It's a tragedy, one that won't soon be forgotten or easily overcome."

The aunts and Brandie just stared at her.

I wondered if she had a public relations firm on retainer who'd whipped up that little speech for her.

"As you can imagine, Patrick is devastated," Julia went on. "He's in seclusion. But he sends his heartfelt condolences to each of you."

They kept staring.

"The police officers have assured me that you will be given an opportunity to make your statements within the next few minutes. Immediately afterwards, you will be taken to the airport for your return flight home," Julia said.

The aunts gasped.

"Andrea," Julia said. "Call the car service and book their airline reservations."

"Wait," Melanie said.

"Yeah, hold on a second," Renée insisted.

"What about the funeral?" Cassie asked.

"Services and internment will be held at the church in her home town," Julia said.

"We can't just leave," Renée said. "It's not right."

"It's disrespectful," Cassie said.

"We haven't even talked to Patrick yet," Melanie said.

"Patrick is with his family," Julia said.

"We're his family, too," Melanie said.

Julia drew in a breath, as if to steady herself, and said, "There is no reason for you to stay. Everything is being handled."

"Well, I'm not leaving," Renée told her.

The others nodded in agreement.

"There are no appropriate accommodations for you," Julia explained.

"We'll stay here," Melanie said. "There's plenty of

room."

Julia drilled the aunts with a don't-you-realize-I'm-better-than-you glare.

"One does not expect staff to remain on the premises following an event of this nature," she said in an if-you-had-any-class-you'd-know-that voice.

"We don't need a staff," Cassie said. "We can take care of ourselves."

"We sure can," Renée agreed.

I thought Julia might actually morph into a block of ice at any second.

"I'll help out," Andrea offered.

Julia turned her how-dare-you glare Andrea's way, so what could I do but say, "And so will I."

"Good," Melanie said. "It's all settled."

Julia's pinched lips indicated that the matter was far from settled, yet good breeding forbade her from pressing the issue.

"Very well," she said and left.

No way was I staying in that room any longer. If the cops wanted to talk to me, they'd just have to hunt me down.

I left and walked down the hallway heading for the front door—and spotted Julia.

Crap.

She walked over, her I-could-pass-for-a-wax-figure composure once again firmly in place.

"I realize my comments may have sounded cold," she said, sounding, of course, incredibly cold, "but I hope you could see that I was attempting to soften the blow."

I had no idea what she was talking about.

"What blow?" I asked.

"The heartache they will endure when the police reveal

that Veronica killed herself," she said.

Oh my God, where had that come from?

"She was an impetuous girl, unfortunately," Julia said. "She didn't think things through. Things such as leaving her home and her family, marrying my Patrick, attempting to assist in the running of a major business venture. She was in over her head here. She was glad her relatives were coming because she intended to go back home with them."

Okay, I was thoroughly shocked.

"But she and Patrick seemed like they were so much in love," I said.

Julia dismissed my words with a graceful flick of her wrist.

"She confided in me," Julia said.

Wow, had I misjudged Veronica's relationship with her mother-in-law, or what?

"But now her aunts and cousin will be here to personally witness the horrifying truth when it's revealed," Julia said, and left the thanks-to-you-and-Andrea unspoken yet heavily implied.

"I can't imagine Veronica taking her own life," I said.

"How could it be anything else?" Julia said. "Even someone so utterly lacking in poise and grace as Veronica wasn't clumsy enough to fall off of a balcony."

Chapter 4

When I walked into the L.A. Affairs office the next morning, Mindy was on the phone jabbing buttons on the console as if she were sitting in front of a video poker machine in Vegas—and looked as frazzled and desperate as a weekend gambler on an all-night losing streak. This didn't make me feel so good about myself.

It was a stretch for me to have patience with Mindy, even under the best of conditions and, really, conditions hadn't been all that great for me lately.

Marcie had told me I'd been kind of crabby and I realized that, as always, she was right—and that no matter how difficult my life had seemed to me lately, it was a heck of a lot better than Veronica's, Patrick's, and their families'.

I decided I should definitely stop acting like such a crab-ass and be nicer.

"Are you ready to party?" Mindy asked, as the lights on her telephone blinked frantically and she held the received away from her ear.

"Yes, I am," I told her, then smiled and went on my way.

I swung by my office and dropped off my handbag—an adorable Chanel tote that perfectly complemented my gray checked pencil skirt and white sweater—and went to the breakroom. Several employees were in there making themselves a cup of coffee, and chatting.

Kayla, my L.A. Affairs BFF who was also an event planner, was heating a muffin in the microwave. She was about my age, tall, with dark hair and a curvy figure.

"What are you doing for Thanksgiving?" she asked.

Okay, this wasn't the best topic for me to discuss so early in the morning—I mean, jeez, I hadn't even had my first cup of coffee yet—especially on the heels of my decision to be a nicer person. Kayla had no way of knowing that, of course. The what-are-you-doing question prior to any holiday was standard among friends and acquaintances.

"My mom is having the family over," I said.

Really, I wasn't sure exactly what Mom had in mind for the day or who she planned to invite—except for some unsuspecting guy who was destined to be set up with my sister. Mom had probably told me the details but I'd drifted off.

"What about you?" I asked, as I got a cup from the cabinet.

"Everybody is going to my aunt's this year," Kayla said. "I have to be at a client's house until mid-afternoon, so the family is holding dinner until I get there."

Wow, that was nice. I had no idea what time Mom was serving but I was pretty sure it would have nothing to do with *my* schedule—more likely the time that she'd assigned to the caterer she'd hired.

"See you later," Kayla said. She grabbed her muffin and coffee, and left.

I filled my cup, added a few sugars and a generous splash of French vanilla creamer, and headed out. At the door I turned back, grabbed two bags of M&Ms from the snack cabinet, and went to my office.

I settled into my desk, sipped my coffee, and got down

to work. First things first, was my policy when starting a new day, so I immediately updated my Facebook page, checked my bank balance, and read my horoscope. I was debating whether to look at the Neiman Marcus or the Nordstrom's web sites for an if-I-don't-find-one-soon-I'll-die handbag when I noticed three phone messages from the day before, all from the same person, someone named Mr. Douglas.

Huh. That was weird. I wasn't handling an event for anyone by that name.

Then it hit me—that was the guy who'd called yesterday wanting an immediate appointment with me to, no doubt, talk about an event for his wife or girlfriend. I'd told Mindy to get rid of him, but he'd called back several more times, it seemed.

Why the heck did he keep calling? Didn't he get the hint?

Yeah, okay, I'd decided just a short while ago to be a nicer person, but that didn't necessarily include spending weeks or months putting together a fabulous occasion for a man desperately in love with someone who wasn't me.

Veronica and Patrick Spencer-Taft flashed in my mind. During the occasions when I'd worked with them prepping the Thanksgiving feast I could see how much they loved each other. And beyond that, they made a great team working side by side at Pammy Candy.

Then an ugly image flashed in my mind. Veronica, distraught and desperate, standing at the glass sliding doors in the master suite of that beautiful mansion, then charging across the balcony, hurling herself over the railing.

Could she really have done that? Could she have killed herself, as Julia had said?

True, Veronica's life had taken a major turn, and I

could see where she might have been overwhelmed by the move, the new house, the business, new friends and family. Trying to fit in when her background was so different wouldn't have been easy.

Could Andrea, as Veronica's personal assistant, been so wrong about her and her relationship with Patrick? Was Julia right and she had been planning to go back home with her family, leave Patrick and everything they'd built? Had Veronica been too unhappy and upset to tell Patrick how she felt?

I didn't like any of those thoughts or images swirling around in my head, so I pushed them out. They might be for nothing, anyway, once the police completed their investigation. Maybe it had been a horrible accident, after all.

No matter what, I figured the Thanksgiving Day feast I'd been putting together for the employees of Pammy Candy was off. Maybe Patrick would want me to plan a memorial service instead.

Not a great feeling.

My office phone rang. Mindy was calling. I mentally repeated my be-nicer vow and answered.

"Hello? Hello? Is this the accounting department?" Mindy asked.

"No, it's not," I said—pleasantly, under the circumstances.

"Haley, is that you?" Mindy giggled. "Oh, jiminy, are you in accounting now?"

"No," I said.

"That's too bad," Mindy said. "You'd make a terrific accountant."

Good grief.

"Bye, Mindy," I said.

"Oh, wait," she said. "Haley, you have a call—no, you have a client. Yes, client. A client who called, then came by—no, a client who came by, then called—"

I hung up—which was the nicest thing I could do.

I had no idea if a client was in the office or on the phone, so I sat there for a minute in case Mindy transferred a call. She didn't, but given her prowess with our phone system—thank God she wasn't working in a missile silo— that didn't necessarily mean anything.

I gave it a couple more minutes, then decided there was a real possibility that a client of mine had showed up without an appointment and was waiting for me in one of the interview rooms. I grabbed a new event portfolio from my desk drawer—I always look smart when I carry it— and headed down the hallway.

All the interview rooms were empty, except one, and— oh my God, who was that guy?

I froze in the doorway. I couldn't move, couldn't think. My heart raced and I felt all jittery inside.

The man seated in front of the desk was handsome—I mean, really handsome. His hair was somewhere between light brown and blonde, combed carefully into place. He had on a very expensive dark suit, a snowy white shirt, and a gray necktie. Even seated I could see he was tall and that he worked out regularly. I figured him for early thirties.

He spotted me and rose from his chair. "Miss Randolph?"

Oh my God, he had the most gorgeous green eyes I'd ever seen in my entire life.

I fought off the I'm-fifteen-again urge to giggle, play with my hair, and act like a complete idiot—not easy, but I pulled it off.

Oh, please, let me have pulled that off.

"Yes," I said, and walked into the room.

He extended his hand and we shook—and all sorts of crazy heat raced up my arm.

"It's a pleasure to meet you," he said. "I'm Liam Douglas."

Oh my God, he had a fabulous name. He was tall and sturdy, but long limbed and athletic, like he could morph into a Marvel superhero at any moment.

"I'm glad I could finally catch you," he said.

Catch me? What the heck was he talking about? Why would he—

Oh, crap.

He was the Mr. Douglas who'd been calling—and I'd been avoiding like the zombie apocalypse—and now he'd showed up here at the office. I'd suspected he wanted me to stage an event for his wife or girlfriend—men never come in here for any other reason—and now I knew I'd been right.

To make matters worse he was really hot looking, so his girlfriend was probably gorgeous. They, no doubt, had a fabulous life and were going someplace romantic for Thanksgiving—not stuck at their mom's house with boring relatives and probably friends they didn't even know, like I was.

How the heck was I supposed to be a nicer person when these annoying things kept happening?

I channeled my pageant-mom's I-can-look-pleasant-even-though-that-ugly-girl-on-the-end-won-first-place, and said, "I'll have one of our other planners help with your event, Mr. Douglas. I can't take on another client right now."

"I'm not a client," he said. "I'm an attorney and I need to speak with you."

Yikes! Was I being sued?

My entire life flashed through my head. Had I done something suit-worthy? Well, yeah, probably—but I was sure I'd covered all of that up really well.

Then Veronica Spencer-Taft flew into my mind. Was this something to do with her death?

"I'm with the firm of Schrader, Vaughn, and Pickett," Liam explained. "We represent L.A. Affairs."

Oh, crap.

"Let's sit down," Liam said.

I took the power seat behind the desk and he returned to the visitor's chair in front of it. He was definitely in attorney-mode, serious and grim—which was kind of hot—as he took his cell phone from the pocket of his jacket and pushed a few buttons.

"A suit has been brought against L.A. Affairs by one of your clients," he said, consulting his phone. He looked up at me. "It's alleged that an assault took place at the event."

An assault?

I had no idea what he was talking about.

"A sexual assault," Liam said.

Oh my God, how horrible. I sank back in my chair, stunned and repulsed.

Something like that had happened at an event I'd planned? Had I missed the need for sufficient security? Was there something I could have done to prevent such a heinous act?

Liam consulted his notes on his cell phone again. "This occurred approximately one month ago. Do you recall the event?"

"I have no idea," I told him. "No idea at all. I didn't know anything like this took place. Why didn't anyone say something sooner?"

"The pregnancy was only recently discovered," Liam said.

I felt ill—like I might really be sick.

"Do you have notes on the event that you could consult?" Liam asked.

"Of course. Anything I can do to help," I said. "What was the occasion? Whose event was it?"

He glanced at his cell phone again. "It was a birthday party at the client's home in Pasadena, hosted by Fritz Amos and Max Sheldon. Do you recognize those names?"

The event sprang into my head immediately.

"Sure, they were two really nice guys," I said, as the details of the party formed in my head. "But it was all men. No women. And it wasn't some wild occasion. It was an afternoon birthday party for their—"

Oh my God. It was a party for their dog. Their *dog*.

"You call two dogs humping in somebody's backyard a sexual assault?" I demanded.

Liam looked up at me

"Is this your idea of a joke?" I slammed my fists on the desk and shot to my feet. "What kind of a sick twist are you?"

He drew back and looked slightly concerned for his safety. Obviously, he hadn't expected this response from me—which made me even madder.

"I sat here riddled with guilt, sickened by the idea, and all along this supposed assault involved a *dog*?"

I'm pretty sure I shouted that.

"And you *knew it*?"

I definitely yelled that.

Liam continued to gaze at me, but he didn't look angry or upset. He looked pleased, or something, and he actually started to grin.

Oh my God, he was *not* grinning.

"I don't give a rat's ass about your stupid lawsuit! I don't care if it costs a billion dollars to settle, I'm not helping you with it! And don't you ever come here again!" I screamed.

I stormed out of the interview room, down the hallway, and into my office. My breathing was labored, my knees shook, and I was on the very edge of perspiring.

I couldn't remember when I'd been so completely furious—with anyone. And that's saying a lot because some of my clients were real jerks—not to mention some of the guys I'd dated, some of the guys my friends had dated, and, of course, my mother.

I stomped to the window and gazed out, desperate to catch a glimpse of something—anything—pleasant so I could calm myself. That Liam Douglas was infuriating and I was close to completely losing control—and just when I'd sworn to be a nicer person.

A minute or two passed while I drew in calming breaths and forced myself to think happy thoughts.

I'm not really good at calming breaths or happy thoughts.

At this point, I realized, nothing would help but a massive amount of chocolate.

I remembered that I'd gotten two bags of M&Ms from the snack cabinet in the breakroom this morning so I whipped around to grab them off of my desk and—oh my God. That horrible Liam stood in my office doorway.

My heart rate shot up at the sight of him—but for a totally different reason this time.

"How can a pregnant woman tell if she's carrying a future lawyer?" Liam asked. "She has an uncontrollable craving for bologna."

I laughed—I didn't want to, but it flew out. I clamped my lips together so I couldn't do it again.

"I'm sorry," he said, and walked into my office. "I handled that badly. When you walked in and I saw you, I …"

"I inspired you to act like a jerk?" I asked.

"You inspired me to stop thinking clearly," he said.

He looked slightly mystified and, of course, so was I. We both just stood staring at each other, then he grinned.

He had a great grin.

Not that I cared.

Really.

"Maybe we can take another run at this some other time?" he asked.

"I don't think so," I said.

His grin got wider—which was really weird—and he simply nodded and left my office.

I staggered to my desk chair and collapsed.

I'd barely caught my breath when my cell phone rang. Jack Bishop was calling.

Oh my God, two totally hot guys within minutes of each other?

I nearly fell out of the chair.

"I just got word from the cops," Jack said, when I answered. "It's official. Veronica Spencer-Taft was murdered."

Chapter 5

Jack waited in the hallway outside the entrance to L.A. Affairs while I walked out. He'd called from the parking garage and asked me to meet him so we could talk in person.

Today he had on jeans, a white dress shirt, and a sport coat, and he looked great. But I noticed a little strain around his eyes that hadn't been there yesterday. I figured he was getting pressure from the Pike Warner law firm on behalf of the Spencer-Taft family to come up with some answers in Veronica's death.

"It's official?" I asked. "She was murdered?"

Jack nodded. "The techs calculated the trajectory of the fall and the body's impact on the patio. It didn't add up. The detectives found a witness, one of the construction workers, who saw her go over the railing. She didn't jump, and it was no accident. Someone pushed her."

Jack didn't give any more details but I could imagine what the scene had looked like. Veronica grasping for a handhold, horror on her face as she tumbled.

Too awful, I decided, and pushed on with another question.

"Did the witness see who did it?" I asked. "Male, female? Old, young? Anything?"

"Nothing," Jack said. He was quiet for a few seconds then said, "Look, I'm heading up this thing. The family wants answers and prefers their own security team over the cops."

This wasn't unusual among the caliber of people who could afford to retain personal security. I knew it meant there was a great deal of pressure on Jack from all sides. Expectations were high. His reputation was at stake.

"With the cops ruling the death a murder," he said, "it could mean the family has been targeted. There's the possibility of kidnapping, extortion, robbery. I've put round-the-clock security on the house but I need more."

"What can I do?" I asked.

"Find out everything you can about the family," Jack said, "especially those relatives who just showed up."

Veronica's three aunts and young cousin had seemed perfectly harmless to me. But was it something more than a coincidence that Veronica had been murdered moments after they arrived?

"Find out everything you can about the staff and what went on in that house, especially on the day of the murder," Jack said.

Normally I would have been thrilled at the opportunity to help Jack with a case—his life is so much cooler than mine—but this time the circumstances were grim, sobering.

"You got it," I told him.

"Stay in touch," he said, then headed for the elevator.

I went back inside L.A. Affairs, grabbed my handbag and the Spencer-Taft event portfolio, and headed out.

* * *

"No way," Andrea said. "No way would Veronica take her own life."

We were standing in the entryway of the Calabasas mansion and I'd flat-out asked her about Julia's assertion that Veronica had jumped from the balcony. Even though Jack had told me the police had concluded it was murder, I wanted Andrea's take on the situation.

"You're sure?" I asked.

"Absolutely," she told me. "Come in. Let's talk."

She led the way down the hall in the west wing of the house, past several rooms—including the one I'd been held hostage in with the family yesterday—and into the kitchen. The place was huge, with miles of cabinets, state-of-the-art appliances, and magnificent tile, granite, and woodwork. Dishes, pots, and pans had been washed and left to dry beside the sink; apparently, the house guests were cooking for themselves.

"Where is everybody?" I asked.

I'd seen no workers at the front of the house when I'd pulled up, but had spotted two of Jack's security team patrolling the grounds. No construction was underway inside the house. It was completely empty and silent.

"I'd booked all sorts of tours and outings for Veronica's family," Andrea explained as she opened the refrigerator door. "None of them were up to sightseeing but there was nothing for them to do here, so they went. I just put them in a limo a few minutes ago."

"I guess Patrick's not staying here?" I said.

I couldn't imagine he'd ever want to sleep in the master suite again.

I wouldn't.

"He spoke to Veronica's family last night," Andrea said. She grabbed a soda and passed it to me. "He's a real mess. He might be staying at his parents' place in Hancock Park."

42

Hancock Park was a very prestigious section of Los Angeles, populated by sedate, wealthy, old-money families, just the sort of location the Spencer-Tafts would call home.

"Or he might have gone back to the house in Culver City that he and Veronica lived in," Andrea said, and took a soda for herself. "They were splitting their time between there and here, depending on which rooms were being renovated."

I didn't like thinking of Patrick alone in the house he'd shared with his new bride, remembering all of their time together, recalling their special moments. Too sad.

"He'd probably be better off at his parents' house," I said.

"That would certainly suit Julia," Andrea said, and opened her soda.

I did the same, took a sip and said, "Julia didn't seem all that thrilled with Patrick's choice in a wife."

Andrea led the way to a worktable and we climbed up onto high stools.

"Veronica was struggling with lots of things, certainly with her mother-in-law," Andrea told me. "But she wouldn't kill herself. She was very secure in Patrick's love. She had plans for this house, plans to expand the candy company. She hoped that Brandie would like it here and want to visit more often, maybe even come here for college."

Okay, that was weird. Julia had told me Veronica intended to leave California and return to her family.

"So she wasn't planning to go back home?" I asked.

Andrea looked shocked. "Of course not. She'd never leave Patrick—but wait."

She looked shocked—which I took as a good sign. But

then she shook her head and said, "No. No, it couldn't be."

"What?" I asked.

"Veronica had some kind of announcement she intended to make on Thanksgiving Day," Andrea said.

"About what?"

"She didn't tell me, but I figured it was about expanding the business, since the employees were going to be here for the feast," Andrea said. She shook her head. "It could have been something personal—but absolutely not that she was moving back home."

"Are you sure?" I asked.

"Positive," Andrea told me.

My belly felt queasy as a thought slammed into my head.

"Do you think maybe … maybe Veronica was pregnant?" I asked.

"Absolutely not. I ran all her errands. I picked up her prescriptions. She was on birth control—and she was a fanatic about it," Andrea said. "She wouldn't have left Patrick and she wouldn't have thrown herself off that balcony."

She seemed certain that Veronica hadn't taken her own life and that she was happy here, yet Julia seemed equally sure that just the opposite was true. Had Veronica told Julia about her plan to leave, and not mentioned it to Andrea? Possibly.

Something hit me then.

"What about Veronica's mom and dad?" I asked. "Why didn't they come out with her aunts and Brandie?"

"Her dad passed away a long time go," Andrea said, "and her mom has some health problems and can't travel."

We sat in silence for a few minutes. I didn't know

how much the police had told the family or how much of it had filtered down to Andrea, but if Jack's concerns were spot-on—and I had no reason to doubt them—everyone in the house could be at risk.

"Did you hear the police had determined the cause of death?" I asked. When Andrea shook her head I said, "Veronica didn't jump from the balcony. She was pushed."

Andrea gasped and pressed both palms to her cheeks. Tears pooled in her eyes.

"She ... she was murdered?" she managed to ask.

I nodded.

She took a few minutes to compose herself, wiped her eyes and sighed heavily.

"Veronica was so full of life, so full of energy. She was one of the nicest, sweetest people I'd ever met," Andrea said.

"Did anything seem unusual about the day Veronica died?" I asked. "Was there anyone here who shouldn't have been?"

"Just the staff," Andrea said. "Two cooks and two housekeepers. But all of them had worked for Julia for years."

"And all of the workmen doing the renovations had been vetted by their employers?" I asked.

"Of course," Andrea insisted. "Nobody running a business that catered to the types of people who live in this area would send anyone to the home of one of their clients without doing a background check. They wouldn't want to be responsible for unleashing a stalker or undercover reporter, or something like that, on them. Anyone who did that would be out of business in a heartbeat."

"Did Veronica seem different in the last week or so?" I

---

asked, and sipped my soda.

Andrea thought for a moment and said, "She'd seemed a little more stressed than usual, but who can blame her? Her family was coming and she wanted to get the house ready for them, and for the Thanksgiving feast she and Patrick were hosting for the Pammy Candy employees. And, of course, there were the usual things everybody deals with at this time of year for the holidays."

Everything Andrea described seemed like normal stuff—except that, somehow, Veronica had been murdered.

Andrea shuddered. "The killer had been right here in this house?"

"That's what it looks like," I said, and Jack's concerns came back to me again. "Listen, you should know there's a possibility the family has been targeted, for some reason."

Andrea didn't look all the surprised. She'd worked as a personal assistant for other high-profile people in Los Angeles, and knew what to expect.

"Maybe it would be best if the family went back home," she said, then shook her head, as if reconsidering her own suggestion. "But we'd have to tell them why. And if word got out?"

We both knew the media feeding-frenzy that would ensue if the story broke—the murder of a young woman from a wealthy family, out-of-town relatives fleeing in panic, and a Calabasas mansion on lock down. The speculation would be endless, the Spencer-Taft family would be furious, and Jack would be held responsible for not keeping an air-tight security lid on the incident.

"Here's what we'll do," I said. "I'll have the security team put a female in the house. You tell the aunts that she's from a concierge service and is in charge of taking them on tours and things. That way they won't become alarmed, but they'll be protected."

I knew Jack would go along with it—and it was totally cool to think I'd come up with a helpful idea.

Not that I'm desperate to impress Jack, or anything. Really.

Andrea nodded. "I can sell that. No problem."

"Are you going to be okay here, keeping an eye on the family?" I asked. "You could be in danger, too."

She shrugged. "I need the work. I'll stay until I'm no longer needed."

I slid down off of the stool and said, "You'll let me know if you recall something out of the ordinary with Veronica, or the family, or anything?"

"Of course," she promised. "I don't know what's up with the Thanksgiving feast for the employees. I'll try to approach Patrick about it soon."

"I'll keep going forward with it until I hear differently."

I dropped my soda can in the recycle bin, then wound my way through the big house and out to my Honda. The white BMW that belonged to Veronica was still parked there, alongside Andrea's Mazda.

My head was full of suspects as I pulled away—not a difficult list to compile, since I pretty much knew everyone who had been at the house the day of the murder.

Julia was there. While she was hardly a loving mother-in-law, she was devoted to Patrick. She knew how much he loved Veronica. They'd been married for well over a year. For Julia to have suddenly lost it and thrown Veronica over the balcony, something major must have happened. I couldn't imagine what it might have been so I knew of no motive—yet she'd disappeared shortly after the family arrived and gone, presumably, into the house.

Erika had disappeared along with Julia. I hadn't actually seen either one of them go inside. Were they together? Had one—or both—of them gone in? Or were they on the grounds overseeing the renovations with one of the workmen?

Erika was the interior decorator. If Veronica was dead she would likely be out of a job, so what could her motive have been for murder?

I pulled up to the security gate. Cars were stopped on the opposite side as the guard consulted his approved list of visitors. It reminded me again how difficult it was to gain access to the area.

The exit gate swung open and I drove through. Yesterday, a murderer had done the same. The mental image gave me a creepy feeling so I forced my thoughts back to possible suspects.

What about Renée? She'd rushed into the house immediately upon arrival, claiming she needed to find a bathroom. She'd been alone inside for a while, then admitted that her search had taken her all over the residence. Did that include the master suite? Could she have dashed upstairs, found it, seen Veronica and pushed her over the balcony?

Sure, it was possible. But why would she do it?

When I'd gone upstairs to find Veronica, I'd heard noise from a work crew nearby. Was one of them some psycho killer, or something, who'd pushed her off the balcony in a crazed fit of rage?

I wondered, too, about the cooks and maids Julia had sent to take care of Veronica's house guests. Andrea said they'd worked for Julia for years and, presumably, were beyond approach.

But they were also devoted to Julia. Would they have done away with Veronica because of some whacked-out sense of loyalty? Could Julia have decided to get rid of her daughter-in-law and somehow gotten them to do her dirty work for her?

Was I stretching for suspects?

Oh, yeah. I was.

My brain definitely needed a boost. The soda I'd had with Andrea just wasn't cutting it so I headed for the Commons, the shopping center that served the upscale Calabasas residents. I knew a Starbucks was there.

I knew where all the Starbucks were.

As so many Southern California days were, this one was gorgeous. I decided I owed it to myself to enjoy the weather a bit—plus, it was a good reason to delay my return to the office—so I parked and went inside.

The place smelled great, of course, and a number of people were scattered around the room, reading, working on a laptop, or chatting with friends as they sipped their coffees. I ordered my all-time favorite drink in the entire universe, a mocha frappuccino, and paid for it with the company's gift card I'd registered online.

I didn't know how the heck I'd missed it, but I'd recently learned that Starbucks had a loyalty program that tracked your purchases—you got a cool star for each one—and awarded special discounts and free items after you'd accumulated a certain number of stars. The whole thing was tracked online. There was even a mobile app. I was within six purchases of moving up to the next level— whatever that was. I hadn't read their web site instructions all that carefully.

That happens a lot.

I got my frappie and look a long sip as I walked outside. Just as I was about to find a table at their outdoor seating area and let my brain rest, Liam Douglas flew into my thoughts.

I didn't really want to like him—he'd been a total jackass—but there was something about him that made me feel shaky inside.

But maybe that was just my frappuccino—chocolate and caffeine could have that effect, couldn't it?

My cell phone rang. Andrea's name appeared on the caller ID screen. A jolt flew though me. Oh my God, had something else horrible happened?

"I thought of something," she said when I answered.

She didn't sound upset, which made me relax a little—or as much as is possible while drinking a frappuccino, making a mental list of murder suspects, and remembering a hot guy.

"This may be nothing," she said. "In fact, I'm sure it's nothing. Really, I shouldn't have even called."

I hate it when people do that.

"What is it?" I asked, and managed to sound patient.

"I don't want to get anyone in trouble," Andrea said. "And I don't want to get myself into hot water."

I knew she—and every other personal assistant who worked for a wealthy family—had signed a confidentially agreement upon accepting employment. Andrea could get sued for divulging info—or worse, ruin her reputation and never get hired again.

"You won't tell anyone I was the one who said it, will you?" she asked.

"I'm great at keeping secrets," I said.

Which was totally true. Just last week Kayla at L.A. Affairs had told me a huge secret—and I'd told hardly anyone.

I could, however, keep my mouth shut about the info Andrea was about to share—if it was, in fact, something that might get her fired.

She was quiet for another few seconds then said, "Like I said, it's probably nothing. But Erika, the interior decorator? She and Patrick used to date."

I took a big gulp of my frappuccino—and I definitely needed it. Oh my God, was this my first solid motive in Veronica's murder?

"They dated—seriously dated?" I asked.

"From what I heard, they were practically engaged—until Patrick made that trip back east and came home married to Veronica."

Oh, crap.

Chapter 6

"This is b.s.," Bella said, peering inside her brown paper lunch sack. "Nothing but b.s."

We were seated at a table in the breakroom at Holt's Department Store, the crappier than crappy place where I had a crappy part-time job as a sales clerk. This was where I'd met my ex-official-boyfriend Ty Cameron.

His family had owned the chain of stores for five generations, and Ty was the latest to be completely obsessed with its operation to the exclusion of everything else—including me. Thus, our breakup.

Other employees were seated at nearby tables eating, talking, or flipping through the vast selection of outdated magazines. Someone had decorated the place with honey-comb turkeys and paper cut-outs of pumpkins and pilgrims. Hanging next to the fridge was a teaser about the mystery merchandise that would be revealed on Black Friday—an old Holt's tradition. There were other posters extolling the wonders of the store's current marketing campaign, the Stuff-It Sale.

Really.

I'd worked here for about a year now and Bella had become one of my BFFs along with Sandy, who sat at the table with us.

Bella, mocha to my vanilla, was saving for beauty school. She intended to be a hairdresser to the stars and practiced different styles—to be generous and because we're besties, I'll call them unique—on herself.

In the spirit of the upcoming Thanksgiving holiday she'd fashioned a pumpkin atop her hair—at least I thought it was a pumpkin. I couldn't be sure—which told me Bella wasn't having her best day.

Really, I guess none of us were having our best day since it was Saturday and we were stuck here for hours instead of out doing something fun.

"What's wrong?" Sandy asked.

Like Bella, Sandy was around the same age as me. She was kind of tall with hair she regularly switched from blonde to red, then back again. Today it was somewhere in the middle.

Sandy always seemed to find the best in any situation—which was kind of annoying at times—except when it came to picking a boyfriend. She'd been dating the same idiot for as long as I'd known her, a tattoo artist she'd met on the Internet who continually treated her bad. For some reason, she didn't see it. She absolutely refused to break up with him—despite my repeated attempts to share my oh-so fabulous good advice.

Go figure.

"Somebody stole my string cheese," Bella grumbled.

She picked up her sack lunch and dumped the contents onto the table. Out came a sandwich, chips, chocolate cookies, yogurt, and string cheese.

"Isn't that string cheese?" I asked—I mean, somebody had to.

"I packed three," Bella declared. "There's only two here."

"Are you sure?" Sandy asked. "Because yesterday I was sure I'd put a bag of Fritos in my lunch but I didn't."

"Somebody stole your Fritos," Bella told her. "Just

like they stole my string cheese."

"Is anything missing from your lunch, Haley?" Sandy asked.

"Besides flavor and nutrition?" I asked, gesturing to the reportedly-ham sandwich I'd gotten out of the breakroom vending machine.

"What the hell is going on at this place?" Bella grumbled. "What kind of person would steal food out of somebody else's lunch sack?"

Sandy leaned in—sensing possible gossip, Bella and I immediately leaned in too—and whispered, "Maybe it was one of the new people."

We sprang into stealth mode, all of us sitting back, darting our gazes around the room at the other employees. With the official kick off of the holiday season coming up, Holt's had hired a ton of new sales clerks. They were all seasonal workers, here only until the first of January.

All the new faces I spotted seated around the breakroom looked as tired and worn out—and kind of shell-shocked—as all of us permanent employees.

Retail work had that effect on people.

If one of them had stolen Bella's string cheese it wasn't readily apparent, not that I could see, anyway.

The breakroom door swung open and banged against the wall. I didn't have to look in that direction to know that Rita, the cashiers' supervisor, had burst into the room.

Rita was about as wide as she was tall—which would have been okay except that she continually dressed in stretch pants and knit tops with farm animals on the front.

Her goal in life was to make lives miserable—especially mine.

"Your lunch break is over, princess," she barked at me.

I hate her.

"I have four more minutes," I told her. It wasn't true, but so what.

"Some kids just dumped half the greeting cards onto the floor," Rita said. "You need to go pick them up."

I was about to make the kindest remark I could think of regarding Rita and what I thought she could do with the greeting cards—it did not involve me picking them up— when a girl hopped up from the table next to ours and said, "I'll do it, Rita. No problem. I was finished eating anyway."

Okay, that was weird.

And disappointing—for Rita, anyway. She glared at me and I glared back—yes, just like eighth grade.

"I'm glad to help out," the girl said. "Anything I can do, just let me know. That's what I'm here for."

"Thank you, Gerri," Rita said. She mad-dogged me until Gerri dumped her trash and clocked-in, and the two of them left the breakroom.

"She's one of the new people," Sandy said.

I figured, because I hadn't seen her before. She was probably early twenties with dark hair, and kind of average in height, weight, and looks.

"What was she eating for lunch?" Bella demanded.

"Gerri's a really hard worker," Sandy said. "We were in the shoe department yesterday and, wow, she was shelving merchandise like a ninja. I think she's hoping they'll keep her on after Christmas, or maybe give her more hours."

"More hours in this place? No thanks," I said.

"I ought to check out her trash," Bella mumbled.

"She probably needs the money," Sandy said. "Especially with Christmas coming up."

I couldn't argue with that. And, really, the income

from Holt's had been a lifesaver when I'd started here last year. I was lucky to have a full time job at L.A. Affairs that paid well, but since my benefits hadn't kicked in yet, I was sticking it out here because of the medical coverage.

Being responsible is inconvenient at times.

My cell phone vibrated in my pocket. I pulled it out and saw that Jack was calling.

"Gotta go," I said, as I sprang out of my chair.

"Must be a hot guy," Sandy said.

"Ask him if he's got a brother," Bella called, as I dashed out of the breakroom.

No way did I want to have a conversation with Jack in front of anyone, so I hit the green button on my phone as I raced down the hallway past the managers' offices and the customer service booth. I pushed through the swinging doors and went into the stockroom.

"The undercover investigator will be in place tomorrow," Jack said when I answered.

He sounded tense, deeply entrenched in private-detective mode—which was way hot.

I'd talked with him yesterday about putting one of his people in the Spencer-Taft mansion for extra security under the guise of someone from a concierge service, and he'd liked it. I was glad he was making it happen.

"Did anything pop on the work crews?" I asked.

"Everybody's clean, so far," Jack said. "Still checking."

I paced through the aisles of the stockroom. It was quiet back here, except for the store's canned music track that played faintly. The shelves were all jammed with Christmas merchandise that would be displayed on Black Friday.

Andrea had told me that Erika and Patrick had dated,

and I hadn't told Jack yet. I wasn't sure if it was old news or something relevant to Veronica's murder, and I hadn't wanted to look like I was just talking crap about Erika— not to Jack, anyway—nor did I want to tell him something he already knew.

But neither did I want to look as if I hadn't come up with anything new that would move the investigation forward—which, I know, was kind of shallow of me, but there it was.

"Did you know that Patrick and Erika used to date?" I asked.

Jack was quiet for a few seconds so I knew this was something he hadn't heard, which was totally awesome because now, for a change, I was the hot one.

I gave him the run down on what Andrea had shared with me, then added, "So I'm wondering if it was really over between Patrick and Erika."

"It must have been, if she was decorating their house," Jack said.

I shook my head as I paced. Men. They really knew so little about the devious ways of women.

"Maybe not," I said. "It could mean she definitely wasn't over Patrick and wanted to get into the house and do away with Veronica. Then she would be in the perfect position to swoop in and take Patrick."

"Who hired Erika?" Jack asked.

"I'm going out there this afternoon," I said. "I'll find out."

"Good," Jack said. He shifted to his Barry White voice and said, "Thanks, Haley."

My breath caught. I'm totally helpless against his Barry White voice.

He ended the call before I could say anything—which

was good, because I couldn't think of anything to say, anyway.

* * *

I hadn't really planned on going out to Calabasas this afternoon but while talking to Jack I'd decided I should. I was worried about Veronica's family, even though Jack had security personnel on the property, and I wanted to check on things personally. Plus, I'd told Andrea I'd help out.

Of course, more info was definitely needed from the family and I figured I would be in a better position to root it out than someone who was investigating the murder in an official capacity. Homicide detectives tended to put people off—or maybe that was just me.

I swung by my apartment after my shift ended at Holt's—my fabulous apartment, which I totally loved, was only a few minutes from the store—and freshened my hair and makeup, and changed into pants and a sweater that were nicer than the jeans and T-shirt I'd worked in all day. I headed out to Calabasas and called Andrea as I merged onto the 101.

"I wanted to come by," I said, when she answered. "Will you let the gate guard know?"

"Sure," she said. "I'll put you on the permanent list."

"How's it going?"

"Okay," Andrea said, then paused a few seconds and added, "but kind of boring, really. They toured Universal Studios yesterday so they're exhausted—the aunts, anyway. This was supposed to be their first full day with Veronica and Patrick, so that's not helping."

"How's Patrick holding up?" I asked.

"He asked me to move into the house while Veronica's family is here, to look after them and try to keep them entertained," Andrea said.

"Wow, that's tough," I said. "Can you do that?"

"For what he's paying me? You bet," Andrea said. "But other than that, I haven't heard anything. Nobody's been here or called."

I figured Patrick would be too consumed with grief—and understandably so—to concern himself with the house guests. He'd done all he could by having Andrea stay with them.

"What about Julia?" I asked. "Hasn't she checked on them?"

"Not once."

Okay, I knew Julia might be upset too, but that was crappy.

"Oh, by the way," I said, shifting into wanna-be private detective mode, "who hired Erika to decorate the house?"

"Veronica," Andrea said.

That surprised me.

"Somebody must have recommended her," I said because, really, Erika didn't work for the kind of decorator service you'd find in your spam folder.

"She was already involved with the renovations when I came on board," Andrea explained. She was quiet for a moment, thinking, then said, "I don't know who suggested her to Veronica. Nobody mentioned it."

"Did she know about Erika and Patrick's past?" I asked.

"Maybe. I don't know," Andrea said. "But I doubt it would have mattered. She was absolutely secure in Patrick's love for her."

Wow, she must have really believed in Patrick.

"I couldn't have tolerated an old girlfriend that close," I said, and felt an age-old wave of jealousy zing though me.

"Me either," Andrea said. "But that was Veronica. She always thought the best of everybody."

Had that led to her murder? I wondered.

"I'll be there soon," I said, and we ended the call.

I wondered, too, if maybe Patrick's love wasn't as all-consuming as Veronica—and everyone else, apparently—thought it was. Had he had second thoughts about marrying her? Had he hired Erika hoping to ignite an old flame? Could the two of them have plotted to get rid of Veronica?

I didn't like to think about that so, luckily, my cell phone rang. Then I saw that it was Mom.

Maybe the call wasn't so lucky an interruption, after all.

"Good news," Mom declared, when I answered.

I didn't need a crystal ball to predict that Mom's good news had nothing to do with me.

"I've found several eligible bachelors to invite to Thanksgiving dinner for your sister," she told me.

I should have my own psychic hotline.

"I've discussed these young men in depth with a number of my friends," Mom went on, "and two of them are extremely promising. Others are less so. One I was forced to disregard completely. I'll keep looking, of course. There's still plenty of time. I'm confident I'll find the perfect man."

Not that I wished anything bad for my sister, but I kind of hoped Mom wouldn't find anyone to set her up with because I didn't want to be the only one there without a date. I could just imagine all the questions I'd get from family members I seldom saw and from whoever else Mom had invited. Some of them knew that I'd dated Ty but probably hadn't learned that we'd broken up.

I didn't want my personal life on parade, fielding questions, seeing the disappointed too-bad-it-didn't-work-out expressions on their faces, then having to listen to their well-intended pep talks about how they were certain the right man for me was out there somewhere and eventually I'd find him.

And as if that wouldn't be bad enough, who knew what Mom would actually serve for dinner? Last year she'd gone with Russian food—although the vodka had helped everybody get through the day much easier.

Then, for some reason, Liam Douglas flew into my head.

Where the heck had he come from? Why was I thinking about him? Him, of all people?

Well, he was incredibly good looking. And, even though he'd been a total jerk when we'd first met, he'd apologized. He'd even told a funny joke about lawyers. That counted for something, right?

"So you think it's a good idea?" Mom asked.

She'd been blabbing on and I hadn't been listening, I realized.

That happened a lot.

I had only the vaguest notion what she was talking about—some trip to Cuba—so what could I say but, "Sure. Great idea."

"Excellent," she told me. "I'll get right on it."

We ended the call as I exited the 101, wound through the streets, and pulled up to the guard house. I presented my driver's license out the window to the guy I'd seen on duty many times, but he waved me off.

"We have you on our permanent list, Miss Randolph," he said.

"Thanks," I said, and dropped my license into my handbag—a darling Gucci tote.

He hit a button that opened the gate. I drove through.

When I swung into the Spencer-Taft driveway a few minutes later I parked between Andrea's Mazda and Veronica's BMW, and got out. All the construction projects remained just as they were when the workers had been called off the job by the police. I spotted one of Jack's security guys nearby.

As I crossed the circular drive, the front door burst open and Renée charged outside. She stopped, turned back, and yelled, "I'm getting what's due me! And to hell with all of you!"

She slammed the door and stomped off around the house.

Good grief. What now?

Chapter 7

I walked into the entryway in time to see Melanie dash up the stairs. Cassie stood at the bottom looking more than slightly upset. She spotted me and heaved a heavy sigh.

"I guess you heard," she said, looking embarrassed but resigned to what had happened, as if she'd been down this road with her sisters many times.

"Must be tough always trying to be the peacemaker," I said.

Cassie shook her head. "Melanie and Renée have never gotten along. I thought it might be different on this trip, but Renée is worse than usual."

"What's she so upset about?" I asked.

"Basically, she's mad that life didn't turn out better for her," Cassie said. "And right now she's blaming it on Veronica."

Okay, that surprised me.

I guess it showed in my expression because Cassie went on.

"It started years ago," she said. "Veronica found our mother's candy recipe in the back of an old cookbook. We'd lost Mom a decade before that, and nobody had bothered with it since she passed on. So, Veronica started making candy."

"Your mom was named Pammy?" I asked.

"Yes, that's what Veronica called the candy, as a tribute to her grandmother," Cassie said. "Mom was a great cook and so is—was—Veronica. She started selling the candy at the county fair and at farmers' market. She got some of the local stores to carry it and she even set up a website to sell it online."

"Sounds like she was working hard at building a business," I said.

"Mostly, she wanted money to finish college," Cassie said. She shifted uncomfortable and glanced away. "Veronica's mother wasn't in a position to pay for her education."

I remembered then that Andrea had told me Veronica's mom had health problems, and figured it must have been something major—and expensive.

"I guess things improved when Patrick came into Veronica's life," I said.

Cassie smiled. "Patrick is a sweetheart. At first, we had no idea who he was or that his family owned so many of the businesses around the county. He never let on how much money he had. When he and Veronica first laid eyes on each other, it was love at first sight. Everybody knew it. It was the sweetest thing."

It did sound sweet, and I couldn't help but wonder what that would feel like.

"Patrick had the wherewithal to build a business around the candy Veronica was making," Cassie went on. "Imagine, our mother's candy being sold all across the country."

"Your family must have been thrilled," I said.

"You'd think," Cassie said. "Everybody was so happy and so proud, except for Renée. She thought that since it was Mom's recipe, all of her children should get a share of the profits."

"Did everyone feel that way?" I asked.

"No, of course not. Any one of us could have picked up that recipe and made the candy. All of us knew about it. We'd even talked about how much we missed Mom's candy," Cassie said.

She seemed to get lost in her memories for a minute, then went on.

"Besides, none of us knew how to build a business. We didn't have any idea how to get started, keep it going, or turn it into something big. Never mind that none of us had the money it would take to get the whole thing up and running."

"Patrick could do that," I said.

"Veronica and Patrick were very generous. They gave everybody money and helped out any way they could. Why, they paid for this trip, every dime of it. But that just made things worse when we got here and a limousine picked us up. Then we pulled up to this mansion. All Renée's talked about was how Veronica's life out here is so grand, and the rest of us are stuck in that same small town we've always lived in."

"What, exactly, did Renée mean when she stormed out of here and said she was going to get what was due her?" I asked.

Cassie rolled her eyes. "I don't know for sure. But I suspect she's got some crazy moneymaking scheme that she intended to spring on Veronica and Patrick. But, well, with Veronica gone I don't know what's going to happen."

"Aunt Cassie?"

We turned and saw Brandie standing in the hallway. I didn't know how long she'd been there or how much she'd overheard, but Cassie didn't seem concerned.

"Can we please go somewhere?" Brandie moaned, in true teenage fashion. "It's so boring here."

"I'm just exhausted," Cassie said. "But Andrea said we were getting our own tour guide tomorrow. There'll be plenty to do then."

Brandie slumped against the wall and sighed. Obviously, tomorrow was too far in the future to satisfy her.

Not that I blamed her.

"Want to go for a drive?" I asked, then added quickly, "If it's okay with your family."

Brandie sprang to life like a missile launched from a naval destroyer, and rushed over. "Can I go, Aunt Cassie? Mom won't care. Can I?"

Cassie glanced up at the second floor, then nodded. "Melanie is probably taking a nap and I don't want to wake her, so, okay, you can go."

"Yes!" Brandie gave a fist pump and headed for the door.

"Don't let her talk you into getting in trouble," Cassie said to me.

I wasn't worried. When it came to finding trouble I didn't need any help—and I knew all the shortcuts.

"We'll be gone a few hours," I said to Cassie.

As I followed Brandie through the front door, I pulled out my cell phone and called Andrea.

"When are you getting here?" she asked as soon as she answered.

"I'm here already," I said. "Where are you?"

"Actually, I'm hiding in the media room," Andrea admitted. "Melanie and Renée got into a big argument. I couldn't take it."

"You're safe to come out," I told her. "Melanie is napping and Renée is outside. I'm taking Brandie for a drive."

"Thank God," she said. "You're a lifesaver."

"Let the security guys know Brandie is with me, will you?" I asked.

The last thing I needed was for someone to think she'd gone missing.

"Sure. Have fun," she said, and we ended the call.

When I got outside, Brandie was bouncing on her toes next to Veronica's BMW.

"Let's take Veronica's car, okay?" she asked. "We can put the top down. It'll be so cool."

The Beemer would definitely have been cooler than my Honda, but no way was I taking it.

"I know where the keys are," Brandie pleaded. "I can drive."

"How old are you?" I asked.

She drew herself up a little and said, "I'm almost sixteen."

I figured that was teenager-speak for almost fifteen.

"I know how to drive," Brandie insisted. "Everybody my age drives, back home."

That was probably true, but her experience on rural two-lane roads was no match for Southern California's freeways.

"Do you have a driver's license?" I asked.

"Well, no," she admitted.

"Then I'm driving," I said, and pointed to my Honda.

Jeez, who'd have thought I would be the responsible one?

We got in and I pulled away from the house.

"I need a Starbucks," I said.

"Is there really one of those places around here?" Brandie asked.

I nearly ran up on the curb.

"You don't have a Starbucks near your house?" I asked.

Oh my God, how could anybody live in a place that didn't have ready access to multiple Starbucks locations?

That alone was reason to move to Los Angeles.

Brandie didn't seem to take offense to my question. She was occupied craning her neck to try and get a look at the houses that were hidden behind the tall trees and thick shrubs that had been planted to keep people from doing just that.

"There's one over in the next town, but it's kind of a long way," Brandie said. "Mom says it's too far to drive to get an overpriced cup of coffee."

That was probably true—but it wasn't the point.

I drove to the Commons shopping center and we parked outside of Starbucks. Inside, I recommended a mocha frappuccino—the world's most fabulous drink—and Brandie went for it. We both got ventis with extra whip cream and double chocolate drizzle.

"Oh my God, this is fabulous," Brandie moaned after the first sip. She pulled her cell phone from her pocket and snapped a selfie. "I'm posting this on Facebook."

I hated to think about Brandie going back home and never enjoying a frappie again. I mean, really, was that any way to live?

"Give me your phone," I said.

She looked as if I'd just asked for one of her kidneys, but finally handed it over. I accessed my Starbucks account and downloaded their app, then handed the phone back to her.

"You can use my account," I said, "and get a drink whenever you want."

Brandie looked down at her cell phone as if it was

suddenly worth its weight in gold—which it kind of was, now that it had a Starbucks app on it.

"And the drinks will be free?" she asked, looking up at me as if I'd taken on rock star status. "You'd do that for me?"

"Sure," I said.

It would be cool to see that she'd used the app and know she was at Starbucks enjoying a drink I'd introduced her to. I knew there was a chance Brandie would go back home and treat all of her friends to multiple drinks at my expense, but if she did I could just cancel the card.

"That is so cool," she told me. "Thanks."

"Have you been to the beach yet?" I asked.

Her eyes got big. "Can we go? Is it far? Can we go now?"

"You bet."

"Oh my God," she whispered.

We got back into my Honda and I drove to the 101, then headed north—which always feels like west to me—and exited on Las Virgenes. Most signs of civilization gradually disappeared as the two lane road wound through the rugged canyons.

Brandie seemed more interested in the scenery and taking pics with her cell phone than talking, which was okay with me. I kept replaying in my head what Cassie had told me.

Renée wasn't happy and blamed it on Veronica, claiming she'd cheated her out of money from the candy business that she felt should be hers. Was that a motive for murder, or what?

I couldn't shake the memory of how Renée had blasted into the house immediately upon arrival, and how she'd been in there alone for quite some time. She'd even admitted she'd been all over the house.

Had she really been searching for a bathroom? Or was that a clever cover story?

And where had Erika been during that same time? She'd disappeared pretty much as soon as the family got out of the limo. Did she think this was her chance to murder Veronica? That having so many new people in the house might create more suspects? Could she have wanted Patrick back in her life badly enough to murder Veronica?

Of course, Julia had vanished at the same time. I had no reason to think she'd want Veronica dead—enough to actually murder her, that is—but I couldn't let go of her as a suspect.

"Oh my God," Brandie said.

I saw then that a slice of the Pacific Ocean had appeared ahead of us between the hills.

"This is awesome," she said.

I was with her on that. Even after living my whole life here, the sight of the ocean was still cool.

We drove down the winding road and I turned left on Pacific Coast Highway at Malibu. Brandie's head swiveled back and forth as she tried to take in the ocean, the stores, restaurants, and businesses that lined both sides of the road.

"Want to get your feet wet?" I asked.

"Of course," Brandie said.

I drove a little further down PCH, then turned right into the parking lot next to the Santa Monica pier. The lot was close to the ocean, and there were restaurants, gift shops, and carnival rides on the pier. I paid the attendant, swung into a parking spot, and we got out.

"No wonder Veronica loves it out here," Brandie said, as she held up her cell phone, taking more pictures.

"She wasn't planning to go back home?" I asked.

"After all the trouble the family put into keeping her big secret from Patrick and everybody?" Brandie said. "No way."

I froze. Oh my God. Veronica had a secret?

Brandie gasped and pressed her lips together.

"I wasn't supposed to say anything," she told me. "Oh my God, Mom is going to throw a complete fit if she finds out I said something."

I didn't want to make things worse for Brandie and I didn't want to get her in trouble with her mom, but I wasn't about to let this slide.

I gave her one of my we're-cool shrugs and said, "You might as well tell me now."

She thought for a second and sighed. "Yeah, I guess."

Brandie didn't say anything—I hate it when that happens then finally drew a big breath and said, "We're not supposed to talk about Veronica's parents. Everybody was afraid that if Patrick knew about them, he wouldn't want to marry her. Like our family wouldn't be good enough, or something. And his parents would be embarrassed and then they'd get a divorce and abandon the candy business. Everybody's life would be ruined."

Now I was dying to know what the secret was, but I knew I couldn't push her.

I hate that, too.

Brandie thought for another minute or so then said, "Veronica's dad abandoned her mom when she was just a baby. He was some total loser, I guess. A druggie, or something. I don't know. The family doesn't talk about him much."

That hardly seemed secret-worthy to me.

"What about Veronica's mother?" I asked.

"That's the thing," Brandie said. She hesitated another moment, then said, "She was a druggie, too. She's in prison."

Oh, crap.

Chapter 8

"This is crazy," Marcie said.

"Yes, but something will turn up," I replied.

We were spending our Sunday morning in the mall at Sherman Oaks continuing our search for a fabulous handbag and, once again, hadn't found anything we loved—or even liked. When we'd done this at the Galleria a few days ago Marcie had suggested I was being a crab-ass about the whole thing. She'd been right—Marcie was almost always right—so today I was making an effort to be upbeat and positive.

"Are you okay?" Marcie asked. "You've been acting weird all day."

So much for the new me.

"Let's try Macy's," I said.

We'd already checked out the Coach and Michael Kors stores, Bloomingdales, and a few other shops. Macy's was our last hope.

"I met this really annoying guy," I said, as we made our way through the crowd. Everything already decorated for Christmas and, apparently, lots of people were getting a jump on their shopping.

"Was he at least good looking?" Marcie asked.

"Totally handsome," I said. "A lawyer. Liam Douglas."

"Sexy name," she said, nodding. "Why was he so annoying?"

I replayed my conversation with Liam in my head and, really, except for the fact that he'd come at me all wrong about my clients and their dog's birthday party, he'd seemed okay. Well, better than okay—but that wasn't the point.

"He made me so mad. I couldn't believe how upset I got. Then he totally backed off and apologized," I said. "I'll never see him again, anyway."

"Too bad. Sounds like you two had some sparks flying," Marcie said. "What are you doing for Thanksgiving?"

Under normal circumstances I would have welcomed a change in topic, but remembering my mom's Thanksgiving Day dinner threatened to throw me into crab-ass-mode again.

"Mom's having people over," I said.

"Oh. Sorry."

Marcie knew about my mom.

"I have an event that day, an afternoon thing. Maybe it will run long and I won't have to go," I said.

Of course, I'd never hear the end of it if I didn't show up and threw off Mom's seating chart.

"Are you hanging out with your family?" I asked.

"Mom hasn't told me what we're doing yet, but we'll probably go to my grandma's again," Marcie said.

Marcie's family was awesome. Her mom was terrific. Honestly, I was always a bit envious.

I thought about Veronica. At least my mom wasn't in prison—and even that didn't make me feel better about my own mother.

My attitude was in a death-spiral, I decided, as we entered Macy's. If I didn't find a handbag here to lift my spirits, desperate measures would have to be taken.

For a couple of months now I'd been putting cash away in my underwear drawer to buy myself something fabulous—I mean, something more fabulous than the fabulous things I often bought myself. What I had in mind was a Louis Vuitton tote. It was an iconic bag offering a host of refinements—from the redesigned interior that featured fresh textiles and heritage details, to the lining in a selection of bright shades that lent a vivid pop of color to the timeless Monogram canvas.

Yes, that was the description on their website.

Yes, I'd memorized it.

How could I not?

I didn't dare mention any of this to Marcie, though. She'd try to talk me out of buying it—right now, at least. She'd explain how Christmas was approaching, how I hadn't had my job performance review at L.A. Affairs that would guarantee me a permanent position there, that the tote cost over three grand, and blah, blah, blah.

Not that I didn't appreciate Marcie's concern for my finances.

Anyway, if I didn't find a handbag I loved—and soon—I was going to break down and buy the Louis Vuitton tote.

When Marcie and I got to the handbag department at Macy's we did our usual search, scoping out the purses in the display cases. We made one lap, then looked at each other and sighed. No words were necessary. This trip had been a total bust.

"Don't you have to get to work?" Marcie asked, glancing at her cell phone.

As if today hadn't been yucky enough, I still had to face several hours at Holt's this afternoon.

Oh, crap.

* * *

The generations-old tradition at Holt's Department Store nixed displaying Christmas decorations until after Thanksgiving—one of the very few retail establishments that celebrated Christmas during the actual Christmas season. Nothing went up until Black Friday.

I didn't know if our customers appreciated the store's we're-Christmas-purists attitude but they sure as heck seemed to like the Thanksgiving Stuff-It sale, I realized as I squeezed through the crowded aisles heading for the employee breakroom to clock-in.

The corporate marketing department had come up with the idea of giving customers a free shopping tote and granting them a twenty percent discount on everything they could stuff into it from our seasonal section. The shelves were filled with canned and boxed foods—gravy, vegetables and, of course, stuffing—and some decorator items.

Thankfully, none of the employees working in that department had been required to dress up in turkey costumes.

When I reached the breakroom, several employees were already lined up and ready to clock-in, while others who'd come in earlier in the day were seated at the tables eating. I stowed my handbag and got in line. Bella came in and went straight to the refrigerator.

"Is it your lunch break?" I called.

"I'm checking on my food," she told me, as she grabbed her lunch sack from the refrigerator. "Nobody better try to take my string cheese again—or anything else. I'm keeping watch."

This seemed like overkill to me, but I didn't say anything. I'd seen Bella angry a few times. No way was I commenting.

I glanced at the schedule hanging by the time clock as I punched in my employee code and pressed my finger to the scanner, and saw that I was assigned to the housewares department. I'd worked there before, and while I didn't love it, I knew that my assignment for the night could have been worse.

Things can always be worse at Holt's.

When I left the breakroom I spotted Sandy straightening T-shirts on a display table in the women's department. Not wanting to miss an opportunity to delay the actual start of my shift, I walked over.

"I think Bella's losing it," I said, and glanced toward the breakroom.

Sandy nodded. "She's been checking on her lunch over and over, all day."

"It is really crappy to steal somebody's food," I said, and picked up a T-shirt so it would look like I was working. I wasn't, of course.

"What are you doing for Thanksgiving?" Sandy asked. Not this again.

"My mom is having people over," I said.

"Moms always decide what everybody is doing for the holidays," Sandy said, folding another shirt. "My mom said my boyfriend could have dinner with us, but he won't."

"Why not?" I asked, and managed to keep the okay-that's-crappy tone out of my voice.

"He doesn't want to meet my family," Sandy explained.

I hate that guy. Sandy deserves somebody so much

77

better.

I drew a breath, forcing myself not to get upset and said, "That must have hurt your feelings."

"Well, yeah, kind of," Sandy said, then gave me a bright smile. "But he's really nice to me most of the time."

Good grief.

"There's no roll-over plan in relationships," I told her.

Sandy looked lost.

"Just because he's nice to you most of the time," I said, "it doesn't make up for him being crappy to you at other times."

She still looked lost.

I gave up.

The aisles were crowded as I snaked my way toward the housewares department, which was also jammed with shoppers. Wading in and straightening stock—while avoiding eye contact with customers—seemed like more than I could manage at the moment. Besides, I had important personal business to attend to and, really, why shouldn't I take care of it on company time?

I cut down another aisle and slipped through the double doors into the stockroom. It was quiet, except for the dreadful music the store always played which was thankfully interrupted from time to time by an announcement over the public address system. I made my way between the giant shelving units, past the mannequin farm, the janitor's closet, and the receiving dock, and bounded up the big concrete stairs to the second floor.

This part of the stockroom wasn't just quiet, it was creepy quiet. The shelving units reached the ceiling and were crammed with small, light-weight items. All of the store's clothing hung from tall racks, each item still wrapped in plastic. There were rows and rows of lingerie and shapewear.

I didn't like coming up here—long story—but it was the perfect spot for me to take care of some personal business since almost nobody came up here at this time of the day.

At the top of the staircase I turned left and found a secluded spot in the back corner between the shelving units. I pulled my cell phone out of my pocket and called Jack. He answered right away.

"Have you talked to Patrick yet?" I asked.

"This morning," Jack said.

He sounded tense. I heard nothing in the background so I had no idea where he was or what he was doing, but I was pretty sure he wasn't hiding out in the stockroom during a crappy part-time job like I was.

I saw no need to mention it.

"He said nothing unusual had been going on in the past several weeks," Jack said. "No unusual phone calls, no strangers showing up at the house or the office, no threats. No problems with anything. Nothing out of the ordinary."

"Did you ask him about Erika?" I asked.

"He said it was over between them."

"Did you believe him?"

Jack was quiet for a few seconds then said, "Yes."

I figured Jack and I were wondering the same thing—would Patrick admit to trying to rekindle a relationship with Erika? Doubtful, when it could be construed as a motive for murder.

"I think maybe Veronica was being blackmailed," I said.

The notion had been on my mind since Brandie had let slip the dirty little family secret about Veronica's mother.

She'd come right out and said that everybody had agreed to keep it quiet, fearing Patrick and his old-money family might be embarrassed enough to bring a halt to their ride on the Pammy Candy gravy train. If that happened, Veronica had more to lose than anyone, making her an ideal blackmail victim.

"Talk to me, Haley," Jack said.

His voice dropped a little—not quite to Barry White frequency, but close.

It was so hot.

"Andrea told me Veronica had been more stressed lately, even with everything that was going on with renovating the house, her family coming out, the candy business, the holidays," I said, then told him about Veronica's mom.

Everyone I'd talk to about Veronica and Patrick claimed that they were hopelessly, deeply in love. Yet I couldn't help but wonder if Veronica questioned just how far Patrick's love would stretch once the hugely embarrassing family secret was made public. The hoity-toity friends of the Spencer-Taft family wouldn't likely give it an oh-well and move on.

"It's possible somebody found out her mom is in prison and was blackmailing her," I said.

"I'm on it," Jack told me and ended the call.

I slid my cell phone into my pocket—I know it's not possible but it actually felt warmer after talking to Jack—and headed for the stairs, then stopped when I heard footsteps. I peeked around the end of the shelving unit and spotted someone walking toward the other end of the stockroom.

It was one of the newly hired sales clerks, I realized, and it took me a few seconds to remember that her name was Gerri.

What the heck was she doing up here? All the seasonal employees shadowed the clerks who ran the registers, bagging merchandise to speed up the check-out lines. I couldn't think of a reason for her to be up here— one that had something to do with actual work.

Then I remembered how she'd jumped up to do Rita's bidding when the greeting cards had gotten trashed. Maybe Gerri really was a kiss-ass trying to get more hours or stay on past Christmas, as Sandy had suggested. Both were real possibilities.

Still, something about it bothered me and I wondered why, exactly, she'd come up here.

Immediately, I shifted into stealth-mode.

I tiptoed down the shelving unit, then cut across the aisles and dropped to my knees watching as Gerri made her way to the lingerie section. She flipped through the panties hanging on the rack, then looked back over her shoulder, pulled two pairs off of their hangers, and stuffed them into her pocket.

Gerri hurried back through the stockroom and skipped down the staircase. I waited until her footsteps faded, then followed her down. As I went through the stockroom doors, I spotted her going into the breakroom. I figured her shift had ended and she was clocking-out so I headed for the store entrance.

I walked slowly—not so slow as to entice customers to ask for help, of course—and reached the door in time to see Gerri go outside. I watched as she crossed the parking lot, got into a white Chevy and drove off.

Oh my God. She stole those panties.

Chapter 9

"Are you ready to party?" Mindy exclaimed when I walked into L.A. Affairs.

I was determined to stay in don't-be-a-crab-ass mode, even though it was Monday morning.

This wasn't helping.

"You bet," I forced myself to say, and kept walking.

Of course, trying to stay upbeat and positive would have been a heck of a lot easier if I didn't have so many major problems on my mind, one of which was what I'd witnessed at Holt's yesterday.

Gerri had stolen merchandise from the store. Granted, it was only two pairs of panties and the company was worth billions, but stealing was stealing. Should I rat her out to the store manager? Or should I let it go?

I wasn't great at letting things go.

Something else troublesome had happened, too. When my shift ended I'd headed home, and while stopped at the traffic light on the corner I'd spotted Gerri's car in the Wal-Mart parking lot. I only noticed it because it was parked close to the street near a couple of RVs.

Why was she shopping at Wal-Mart when she had an employee discount at Holt's? Of course, Wal-Mart carried lots of things that Holt's didn't so maybe it was no big deal. But I couldn't help wondering if Gerri was inside shoplifting bras to go with the panties she'd taken from Holt's.

As I walked passed the cube farm and turned down the hallway toward my office, I decided it was too much to contemplate for so early on a Monday morning. I needed coffee to give my day a boost.

I slipped into my office to drop off my handbag and—oh my God. A man was sitting in front of my desk and—oh my God, it was Liam.

He shot to his feet.

Oh wow. He looked great. Today he had on a charcoal gray suit, and a shirt and tie in pale shades of blue. And those green eyes of his. Oh my God.

"What do you call two hundred lawyers at the bottom of the San Francisco Bay?" Liam asked. "A good start."

He smiled.

I smiled—and I giggled. I couldn't help it.

"I hope you don't mind me dropping by," Liam said.

I resisted the urge to keep smiling and giggling, and pulled myself together—not easy with no coffee yet today.

"I wanted to let you know the lawsuit is settled," he said. "I thought you might be worried."

"I wasn't worried," I said.

"Oh. Well, good. I wouldn't want you to worry," he said.

"That's why you came here?" I asked. "That's kind of lame."

"I know," he said, then grinned. "But it was the best excuse I could come up with on a Monday morning."

"Monday's are tough," I agreed.

We looked at each other for a few minutes, then he walked past me to the door. Wow, he smelled great.

"I'll find a better excuse for tomorrow," he told me, then left.

I stood frozen in place for a few seconds, then leaned

out my office door. Liam stood at the end of the hallway, waiting, looking my way.

What nerve. He thought I would come out of my office to catch a last glimpse of him.

I had—but that's not the point.

Liam smiled—it was kind of a cocky smile, but I guess I deserved it—then waved and walked away.

Oh my God. Now I desperately needed a giant infusion of sugar, chocolate, and caffeine. I headed for the breakroom.

* * *

I'd barely calmed down from seeing Liam—the coffee and two chocolate doughnuts helped—when my cell phone rang. I saw Andrea's name on the caller ID screen and answered right away.

"Is everything okay?" I asked, as I rose from my desk chair and walked to the window.

"Well, yes, it's just that …" Andrea paused, then said, "Something been bothering me and I don't know what to do about it."

I waited.

I'm not good at waiting.

"Earlier last week I overheard Veronica and Patrick," Andrea said. "They were arguing."

Okay, that surprised me.

Andrea must have read my mind because she said, "I know, it was totally unlike them. And it could have been nothing, but it stuck in my head."

"What were they arguing about?" I asked.

"I couldn't hear what they were saying, just their raised voices," Andrea said, then paused for a few seconds. "You don't think it had anything to do with Veronica's death, do you?"

Several possibilities shot through my head. Maybe Veronica had told Patrick she planned to return home with her relatives. Or maybe Patrick had confessed that he and Erika were getting back together. There was also the possibility that it had something to do with the big Thanksgiving Day announcement.

"I mean, no way would Patrick hurt her—kill her—and he wasn't even there that day," Andrea said. "Should I tell the police? I guess I should, but I don't want to get Patrick in trouble."

I didn't see this as a big clue that would break the case wide open, more like something that might distract the homicide detectives and lead them down a dead end. But I understood how Andrea felt.

"Hold off for a few days," I said. "See what the detectives turn up and if they don't find a suspect, you should think about telling them."

She sighed. "That's a good idea. Thanks."

"How are the house guests?" I asked.

"Still sniping at each other," Andrea said, and sounded a little weary.

Family—even someone else's—can do that to you.

"I'll try to get out there this afternoon," I said.

"Great," she replied, and we ended the call.

I stood staring out the window for a few minutes thinking about what she'd said about the two supposed love birds fighting, and decided I needed to try and get some inside info on the investigation. I scrolled through my cell phone address book and called Detective Shuman, one of LAPD's finest.

I'd known Shuman for a while and we'd had some ups

and downs—more ups, luckily. He was a little older than me, handsome in a guy-next-door kind of way. There was something between us, kind of romantic, but not really—it was weird.

His voicemail picked up. I left what I thought was an oh-so-clever message about needing info on Veronica's murder investigation that I hoped would inspire him to call me back with some intel. Next I called Jack to see if he'd learned anything new. His voicemail picked up also so I left a message with him.

I stood by the window staring at my phone. It didn't ring. Neither hot guy called me back. That meant there was nothing else I could do at the moment—except actual work.

I hate it when that happens.

* * *

The office phone on my desk rang. I glanced at my wristwatch and saw that several hours had past.

Wow, time went by fast when you were actually working.

"Haley? Haley?" Mindy asked when I answered. "Hello? Can I speak to Haley?"

"I'm Haley," I said.

"Oh, jiminy, so you are!" Mindy giggled. "You have a client. Oh, of course you have a client—you have lots of clients!"

She laughed at her own joke then wound down and said, "Anyway, you have a client here. Here in the office, that is."

Liam flew into my head. Had he come back?

My heart started to beat a little faster.

"He's in interview room number two," Mindy said. "Two. Yes, it's two. Or maybe one. No, it's definitely two."

I told her thanks—at least, I meant to—and hung up.

I yanked open my desk drawer, checked my hair and makeup in the mirror I kept in my handbag, and hurried out of my office.

Oh my God, was Liam back? He had a way of dropping by unannounced. He'd been here once today already. Why would he come back?

A dozen reasons zinged through my head—most of them involving how fabulous he hopefully thought I was—as I hurried down the hall to interview room two. I paused, composed myself as much as I could, and walked inside.

Oh my God.

Patrick Spencer-Taft sat in front of the desk.

Every ounce of yay-for-me drained away and I felt kind of ashamed for thinking of myself when Patrick—and so many other people—were going through really rough times.

He looked up when I walked in and got to his feet. He moved slowly, as if all the life had gone out of him.

Patrick was a good-looking guy. Tall, with dark wavy hair, a nice build, and an easy smile. Only right now he wasn't smiling, and he looked as if nothing was easy for him.

He stepped forward and we hugged. I wanted to say how sorry I was about Veronica but he waved me off, as if another condolence was more than he could bear. I took the chair beside his, and we sat down.

I figured he was there to tell me the Thanksgiving feast he and Veronica had been planning was off. I'd expected as much. It would be incredibly sad to plan a memorial service for her but if that's what Patrick wanted, I'd do it.

We sat in silence for a moment before he spoke.

"Thank you for helping out with the family," he said. "I appreciate it, and I know … I know Veronica would have, too."

I couldn't think of anything to say, so I just nodded.

"I want to go ahead with the Thanksgiving feast," he said. "Veronica would have wanted it. She loved Pammy Candy and all the employees who worked there. We promised them a special day and she wouldn't want to let them down."

I still couldn't think of anything to say.

"She felt the business brought happiness to everyone who worked there and to everyone who ate the candy," Patrick said. "I'd like to do this as a tribute to her. A day of thanks for loved ones, good health, jobs, friends, and family."

"Veronica told me several times how much she loved the company you two were building," I said.

"She had plans—big plans," Patrick said, and managed a weak smile. "She wanted to expand the factory and put in a gift shop, have tours, put in a café for the customers."

"Sounds great," I said.

Patrick nodded, then turned away and rubbed his eyes. He was quiet for a moment before turning to me again.

"I just don't understand," he said, and sounded truly lost. "How could this have happened? Who would want to hurt her?"

He didn't, of course, expect me to come up with an answer but since he seemed to want to talk about it, I decided to see if I could get any useful info.

"Was anything unusual going on?" I asked.

Patrick shook his head. "Nothing different. The same kind of things that had been going on for weeks."

"Did Veronica seem upset?"

"No," Patrick insisted. "Well, yes, a little."

"Did you two disagree about something? Argue, maybe?"

He uttered a bitter laugh. "The only thing we ever disagreed about was money."

Okay, that surprised me. Patrick was a multi-millionaire. He hadn't struck me as a tight-wad, but maybe I'd misjudged him. Before I could ask, he went on.

"She was always afraid she was spending too much money," Patrick said, and smiled as if it were her most endearing quality. "I told her to stop worrying, we had plenty of money. But, well, she came from a family that struggled financially. Lately, she even went out of her way to give me long explanations about what she was doing with the money."

"For the house renovations?" I asked.

"No, it was for her personal things. Clothes, spa treatments, her hair and nails. That sort of thing," Patrick said. "It seemed to bother her more lately. She kept telling me how much she loved me, as if she were worried about our marriage. I didn't care how much she spent. I just wanted her to be happy."

I understood Veronica's concern over money, especially given her background, but she and Patrick had been married for over a year. It was odd that she was suddenly distressed about money, and worried that Patrick would be upset with her over how much she was spending.

"Did this have anything to do with the Thanksgiving Day announcement?" I asked.

Patrick took a few seconds to process my question,

then shook his head.

"I don't know anything about an announcement," he said. "Please go ahead with the feast, as planned. Veronica would have wanted it, and I want our employees to know the company will continue despite … despite everything."

"Of course," I said.

"A couple of friends have offered to handle the last minute details," he said. "Andrea knows about them."

"I'll contact her right away," I said.

Patrick sat there for a few more seconds as if trying to muster the energy to rise. Finally he got to his feet.

"Thank you, Haley, for everything."

"Don't worry," I said. "I'll make sure everything is perfect for the feast."

He managed another small smile, and left.

I wondered what announcement Veronica intended to make. Patrick didn't know anything about it, giving me the icky feeling that she'd withheld it from him. I could only imagine why.

I couldn't stop thinking about Veronica's apparent guilt over the money she was spending on personal things. Was that, in fact, what she was spending money on?

Or was she skimming cash out of their joint account to buy a plane ticket back home?

Or maybe pay a blackmailer?

Chapter 10

By late afternoon I'd done all the work I could stand for one day, mostly making sure everything was set for the Spencer-Taft Thanksgiving feast, so I headed out to Calabasas. When I pulled up in front of the house, I saw that Veronica's BMW was no longer parked in the driveway and figured someone had finally put it in the garage. I hoped that meant things were getting back to normal—or as normal as they could be under the circumstances.

I'd called Jack and Shuman during the drive over—the 101 was always a crawl at this time of day—but neither of them answered. I'd tried Marcie next and had passed a few stop-and-go miles discussing our next move in the there-has-to-be-one-out-there-somewhere handbag search. We were running out of places to shop.

My last-resort Louis Vuitton tote was looking better and better.

Andrea met me at the door. She looked a little weary, as if her personal assistant job had turned into a babysitting assignment.

"Patrick found out Julia had pulled the cooks and housekeepers," she said as we walked into the entryway.

I figured Julia had sent the staff packing, thinking Veronica's family would leave sooner if forced to fend for themselves. I wasn't sure why Julia cared one way or the other. She hadn't exactly taken over the hostessing duties.

"That was crappy of her," I said.

Andrea nodded and said, "The agency sent people over so things are a little more bearable now."

"No more arguments between the sisters?" I asked.

"If only." She rolled her eyes. "Makes me glad I'm an only child."

"Are they home?" I asked.

"I'd lined up a winery tour and tasting for them in Temecula today but they cut it short and came back early. Everything seems to wear them out. All but Brandie, of course," Andrea said. "Everyone who isn't napping is at the pool."

We headed toward the rear of the house and I said, "Patrick came by the office today and told me he wants to go ahead with the Thanksgiving feast."

She nodded. "I'll text you the names of the friends who want to help with the details."

We entered a large family room with floor-to-ceiling windows that featured a view of the pool and spa, set among lush landscaping. The room had tile floors, comfy furniture, a wet bar and mini kitchen, and beach-themed décor. Outside, Brandie lay on a float in the pool. Melanie was stretched out on a chaise in the shade.

"I have to make some calls," Andrea said. "The construction crews should have been out here already. There's still a lot to do before the feast."

I walked outside into the glorious Southern California weather. Melanie and Brandie spotted me at the same time.

"Oh my God, Haley, you're here," Brandie exclaimed and rolled off of her float into waist-deep water. "Let's go to Starbucks, okay?"

It sounded like a great idea. I should have stopped on

my way over but I'd been too consumed by my conversation with Marcie—that's how upset I was about not finding a fabulous handbag.

"Oh, you and that Starbucks," Melanie complained. "That's all I've heard about lately."

Brandie shot her mother a resentful look, then dove into the water and swam toward the far end of the pool.

Melanie got to her feet and walked to where I stood by one of the umbrella tables.

"All she wants to do is go places," she complained. "She thinks we can just call the limo anytime we want and be squired around town. She has a pool, a spa, gardens to walk in, a media room, everything, and it doesn't suit her. She wants to get one of those Starbucks drinks and act like she's a California girl like you see on TV."

I thought Brandie's idea was a great one.

This didn't seem like a good time to mention it.

Melanie watched her daughter swim laps for a moment, then turned to me again and sighed heavily.

"You really haven't caught any of us at our best, Haley. This thing with Veronica, well, it's turned us into something we're not."

"It's a tough time for everyone," I said because, really, it was.

"That's no excuse," Melanie insisted. "I'm sorry you had to witness the tail end of that argument I had with Renée. She's been worse than ever on this trip."

Since Melanie had brought up the incident, my maybe-this-will-result-in-something-that's-good-for-me instincts took over.

"What was that all about?" I asked.

"Another one of Renée's big ideas," Melanie grumbled. "She was always coming up with some sort of business scheme she wanted Veronica and Patrick to buy into."

"To make up for the candy business?" I asked.

Melanie nodded. "This time she wanted them to front the money to manufacture those fanny packs."

Yikes! Fanny packs had had their moment a number of years ago. While there was nothing wrong with them and they were indeed functional, the market for them would be very limited.

"Renée had the idea of making one for every season," Melanie said. "She had us all wear them out here to demonstrate how great they looked."

I remembered seeing all the gals wearing them when they got out of the limo—bright orange with bedazzled turkeys on the front.

Not exactly a fashion statement I envisioned catching on.

I wasn't sure how Veronica would have felt about them. She dressed in fashion-forward clothing but I knew she had a stylist who helped her. Of course, if she felt guilty about the Pammy Candy situation, she might have gone along with the idea just to appease Renée.

"Had Renée talked to Veronica about the fanny packs before you arrived?" I asked.

"Of course," Melanie said. "She practically ran over Veronica with the idea, sent her emails and text messages with design ideas and photographs of the bags she'd had a local company make. She thought it was the least Veronica and Patrick could do after they stole the candy business right out from under--"

She stopped and pressed her lips together, realizing she'd said too much.

"Cassie told me," I said, to ease her embarrassment.

94

Melanie looked as if this didn't surprise her, either. "Well, none of it matters now."

With Veronica gone, I couldn't see Patrick investing money in, and heading up, a manufacturing company—especially one that turned out seasonal, bedazzled fanny packs.

"Of course, Renée could have been right and they might have caught on," Melanie said. "It's just one more thing we'll never know the answer to. This trip has been filled with what-ifs."

It took a few seconds before I realized what Melanie was saying.

"You mean Veronica's announcement?" I asked.

She brightened. "Did she tell you what it was?"

"No," I said. "Somebody mentioned it."

Melanie looked disappointed. "I guess we'll never know. All I can do is wonder. You know, that kind of thing—the not knowing—really gets to me."

It was getting to me, too, because I couldn't help but feel as if it had something to do with Veronica's murder. Did it involve Pammy Candy? Or something personal?

Yet how personal could it be if Veronica hadn't told Patrick? When I'd brought it up at L.A. Affairs, he hadn't known anything about it.

At least now I could delete Renée's name from my list of suspects. She wanted Veronica alive and well to start her fanny pack business. No way would she have killed her.

That left me with three suspects—Julia, who had no motive that I'd uncovered; Erika who might, or might not, have been trying to get Patrick back; and a blackmailer who, at this point, was just a figment of my imagination.

Crap.

* * *

When I left the Spencer-Taft house, I called Marcie.

Really, there are times when only your BFF will do.

We decided to meet at a bar downtown near the bank where she worked.

Really, there are times when only wine will do.

Since I was driving against the heavy traffic coming out of Los Angeles, the commute didn't take as long as I'd thought. I parked in a lot and headed up Figueroa Street. Marcie wouldn't be off work for a few more minutes, so I sent her a text letting her know I'd arrived and would meet her at the bar.

We'd met there before so I knew it was an upscale place that attracted a business-suit clientele, and I'd be safe sitting alone until she arrived—not that I expected to be surrounded by hot looking guys wanting to buy me drinks, but, really, it would be nice.

My cell phone rang. I pulled it from of my handbag and stepped out of the flow of pedestrians on the sidewalk. Jack was calling.

Oh, yeah. My day had just improved considerably.

"What have you learned?" he asked when I answered my phone.

Jack sounded tense, all-business. He had a lot on him. A great deal was at stake. He was depending on me to help solve this case but, really, I hadn't come up with anything spectacular that could break it wide open.

Not a great feeling.

"I'm working a few leads," I said, hoping that speaking in accepted private investigator lingo would make it sound as if I'd actually accomplished something.

I rushed ahead with a question just in case.

"Did you uncover anything on the possible blackmailer?" I asked.

"No, nothing," Jack said. "Keep digging."

"I will," I promised, and we ended the call.

I slid my phone into my handbag and continued down the sidewalk toward the bar.

Detective Shuman still hadn't returned my call. Hopefully that meant he was busy gathering info about the murder through his LAPD contacts, and would be in touch soon.

The bar was dimly lit and humming with conversations and the clinking of glasses when I walked in. I snagged a high table in the corner. When the waitress came over, I ordered.

I'm a real stickler for not drinking and driving, so usually I have soda or juice. But after the day I'd had, I figured I could make an exception and have a glass of wine.

My cell phone rang. It was my mom.

One glass of wine wasn't going to cut it.

"Great news," Mom announced when I answered.

Luckily, the waitress brought my wine so I didn't have to say anything.

Not that it mattered.

"I've found the perfect man," Mom declared. "Your sister is going to be thrilled with him."

I doubted it, but didn't say so. Instead, I gulped down some of the wine.

"He comes from a wonderful family, he's a great dresser, and he has a good job," Mom said.

Yet he was willing to be set up on a blind date on Thanksgiving?

Sounded like a major red flag to me, but Mom didn't ask my opinion

I downed more wine.

"Of course, there's another man who's been recommended also," Mom said. "I'm considering both of them."

Mom kept talking—and I kept drinking—so everything she said turned into blah-blah-blah until I heard her say, "So I'm really thinking Cuban. Doesn't that sound wonderful?"

My sister's date would be Cuban?

"Sounds great," I said—which was kind of bad of me, I know, but what else could I say?

I drained my glass and asked. "What time are you serving?"

"Two o'clock," Mom said.

The Spencer-Taft feast was going to be served at noon, so there was a chance I'd be delayed and wouldn't make it to Mom's on time—if I was lucky, that is.

"I'll keep you informed," Mom promised, and we ended the call.

I reached for my wine glass, then saw that it was empty. Jeez, when had that happened?

Just as I was searching the crowd for the waitress, a fresh glass appeared on my table. I looked up and saw that Liam had placed it there.

"Here," he said, and pushed the glass closer. "Drink this until I start to look good."

"I'm going to need another one of these," I told him.

He grinned.

Liam had a great grin. He looked great, too, dressed in a navy blue pinstriped business suit and a maroon shirt and tie combo, holding a beer.

"What's black and brown and looks good on a lawyer?" he asked. "A Doberman pinscher."

I gave him his grin right back—which I sincerely hoped was as hot as his was.

"How do you stop a lawyer from drowning?" he asked. "Shoot him before he hits the water."

Okay, now I laughed. He laughed, too, then gestured to the empty wine glass.

"Rough day at the event planning business?" he asked.

Jeez, he must have seen me chugging it down when I was on the phone with Mom—not exactly the image I wanted to project.

"I was just finalizing some plans for Thanksgiving," I said.

"Family or clients?" he asked.

He sat down in the chair next to mine. Wow, he smelled great. Some kind of heat was rolling off of him, somehow urging me to snuggle closer—even though I hadn't touched my second wine yet.

"I'm staging a feast out in Calabasas," I said, "then going to my mom's house."

He nodded. "My mom's got the whole family going somewhere, doing something. She hasn't told me where I'm supposed to show up yet. Probably my grandma's in San Diego."

I thought it was kind of cool that he was spending the holiday with his family and seemed to be okay with it.

Obviously, his family was more fun than mine.

"Hi there," Marcie said.

I realized she'd joined us at the table. Liam stood and held the chair while she sat on the other side of me. They introduced themselves.

"I should have known I wouldn't be lucky enough to

catch you here alone," he said to me, and favored both of us with a smile. "You ladies enjoy your evening."

Liam gave me one last long, lingering look—or maybe that's how I looked at him—then joined a group of men standing at the bar.

"Oh my God," Marcie whispered. "He's gorgeous."

I tried for a nonchalant shrug, but didn't pull it off.

"Did he ask you out?" she wanted to know. "You'd be crazy not to—"

Marcie suddenly latched onto my arm with a something-major-is-going-down death-grip, and leaned closer.

"Ty's here," she told me.

All my senses jumped to high alert.

Ty Cameron, my ex-official-boyfriend was here? In this bar? Just steps away? Oh my God, why hadn't I noticed him?

And more importantly, why hadn't he noticed *me*?

I shifted into stealth mode and swept the bar. The place was packed with good looking men dressed in expensive suits, crowded together at—

Oh my God, there he was, looking as handsome as ever, impeccably dressed, seated with two other guys. I was relieved he wasn't with a date, but concerned that he was here.

Ty was a workaholic. At this time of day he was usually still elbow-deep in the running of the Holt's Department Store chain, plus its other holdings. Ty definitely wasn't the kind of guy to knock off early, head for a bar, and belt down a few with his buddies.

What the heck was going on with him?

"Do you think he saw you talking to Liam?" Marcie whispered.

My emotions spun up even higher.

Had Ty seen me? Would he come over? Talk to me?

Was he wondering who Liam was? Why I was talking to him? If he was my new boyfriend? Was Ty positively green with envy, re-thinking our breakup, yearning to cross the bar and confront Liam?

Oh my God, were the two hottest guys in the bar about to throw down in an all-out brawl over me?

"You're cut off," Marcie said.

She'd known what I was thinking, as only a long-time bestie can.

And she was right, of course.

I pushed my wine glass away.

Chapter 11

"You only call me when you want something," Shuman said.

"At least I'm calling you," I pointed out.

We were sitting at an outdoor table at the Starbucks on restaurant row at the Galleria having coffee. As soon as I'd arrived at L.A. Affairs this morning, I'd gotten a text message from him asking if I could leave work and meet him here.

I can always leave work.

Shuman had left work, too, it seemed. He was dressed in his usual slightly mismatched sport-coat-shirt-tie combo that told me two things—he didn't have a new girlfriend yet, and he should let me take him shopping.

Neither seemed likely to happen.

Shuman looked calm and relaxed, which I was happy to see. He was a homicide detective, so his day could take a dive at any moment. I was glad I'd caught him early.

"I talked to the detectives investigating the Spencer-Taft murder," he said.

Usually we had to play a who's-going-first game with our information but since he hadn't caught the case, I figured he wasn't all that concerned about sharing what he'd learned.

"There's no progress in the investigation," he said.

Not exactly what I was hoping for.

"No more witnesses, no evidence, and no motive,"

Shuman said.

"What about the workmen and the household staff?" I asked.

"No one with a criminal background. No apparent motive," he said.

Even though Shuman hadn't pressed me for information, I wanted him to know that I didn't intend to withhold anything. I gave him a rundown of what I'd learned from the family and what I suspected—none of which was anything conclusive.

Still, he listened to everything and I could see him running the info through his cop-brain. After a couple of minutes he shrugged. I knew what that meant—something major was going to have to happen if this case was going to be solved.

"So, what are you doing for Thanksgiving?" Shuman asked.

At this point I was as anxious to change the subject as he was so I said, "Doing the family thing. You?"

"I don't know yet," he said.

I didn't think he was the kind of guy who'd sit in front of the TV in his underwear watching football or a Dirty Harry marathon all day but, honestly, it didn't sound so bad—as long as he was really okay with it.

For a few seconds I considered inviting him to Mom's for dinner, but she'd likely freak out if I threw off her seating chart. Plus, it would bring up questions about my breakup with Ty and the inevitable are-you-two-serious speculation. I wouldn't put Shuman through that.

No way did I want to endure it, either.

Shuman must have figured out what I was thinking— he was, after all, a detective—because he said, "A couple of the guys at work invited me to eat with them. I'll probably—"

He pulled his cell phone from the pocket of his sport coat and glanced at the caller ID screen.

"I've got to take this," he said, getting to his feet and instantly transforming into super-serious-cop-mode.

"No problem," I said. "I should get back to work."

We exchanged a quick wave and I headed back to L.A. Affairs.

* * *

"You want to do—what?"

I said it nicely—or as nicely as I could, under the circumstances.

I was seated in one of the L.A. Affairs' interview rooms. Across the desk from me were the two girls who'd volunteered to wrap up preparations for the Pammy Candy Thanksgiving feast. They were pretty much interchangeable—mid-twenties, blonde, full on makeup, spandex dresses, and four-inch pumps—except for their names, of course, which were Sasha and Poppy.

I'd already forgotten their last names.

I was also a little confused about who was who.

"Like I said," the one I'd decided to think of as Poppy told me, "I think it would be a terrific idea if the Thanksgiving feast was strictly vegan."

"Well, if you're going to do that," Sasha said, "I think you should be sure everything is gluten free."

"And sugar free," Poppy said.

The feast was set for the day after tomorrow. Did they really think I could make major changes at this late date?

"Or we should only serve authentic foods," Sasha said.

Apparently so.

"You know," she went on, "like at the first Thanksgiving—venison, collards, parsnips, cabbage, spinach. I read it on the Internet."

I wondered if she'd read on the Internet about an event planner who'd gone over the desk after a client who wanted to completely change the menu two days before the party.

Or maybe that was just wishful thinking on my part.

"Oh, I know!" Poppy said, bouncing in her chair. "All the guests should come in costumes. How fun would that be?"

"I love it," Sasha declared. "Some can be dressed as pilgrims and some can be Indians."

"But we should be culturally sensitive. So only those guests with a verifiable Indian heritage can come as Indians," Poppy insisted, then said to me, "You can do that, can't you? Check that out?"

I didn't say anything. Really, what could I say?

"That's a good idea," Sasha agreed. "Oh, I know! We can get members of the Wampanoag tribe to come. They were at the very first Thanksgiving. I read that on the Internet, too."

"They can do an interpretive dance," Poppy exclaimed. "And to make it even more authentic we'll have wooden tables, and we'll have the caterer cook everything over a big open fire."

"You know what else I read on the Internet?" Sasha said. "Back then, there were millions and millions of passenger pigeons just flying around everywhere. We could get some actors to put on a play, sort of like an ode to the passenger pigeon."

"I love it!" Poppy told her.

They both turned brilliant smiles on me.

"This is going to be the best Thanksgiving ever," Sasha declared.

"You can get all of that handled by Thursday, can't you?" Poppy asked.

I managed an I'm-getting-paid-so-I-won't-say-what-I-really-think smile, and said. "I'll see what I can do."

"Great," they said in unison, and rose from their chairs. Then something hit me.

"Who asked you to take over preparations for the feast?" I asked.

"Julia," Poppy said.

"Patrick's mother," Sasha added.

Did Julia pick an odd time to get involved with the feast, or what?

The two of them left and I headed back to my office.

Jeez, there must be some way I could find one—or both—of them guilty of Veronica's murder so I wouldn't have to deal with them again.

My day desperately needed a boost so I went to the breakroom, poured myself a cup of coffee—generously flavored with multiple packets of sugar and French Vanilla creamer—and took it to my office. Since I'd had so much actual work to do this morning—and not counting my meeting with Shuman—I 'd been forced to put off my usual get-the-day-off-to-a-great-start activities—updating Facebook, checking my bank balance, and reading my horoscope.

I sat down in my desk chair, sipped my coffee, and something flew into my head.

The thing about the big announcement Veronica planned to make on Thanksgiving kept bothering me. I couldn't shake the notion that it had something to do with her murder.

Nobody seemed to know what it was, exactly. There was only speculation that she was leaving Patrick and moving back home. Yet most everyone had insisted Veronica loved him too much to ever leave, and Patrick hadn't even known Veronica intended to announce something.

I sipped more of my coffee and the caffeine and sugar sent different possibilities zinging through my head. I came up with all sorts of ideas, but they were just that, ideas.

Then something else hit me.

Maybe the announcement didn't concern Veronica so much as it did Patrick. Maybe something was going on with him that she wanted to tell the family about.

I got a weird feeling.

Maybe it was Patrick who wanted a divorce.

I popped out of my chair and walked to the window. My brain was buzzing pretty good now as I tried to fit things together in this whole new way.

The notion that Patrick wanted to end things seemed contrary to everything I'd heard about their marriage. But with nothing else to go on, I had to look at things from a different angle—and they didn't get much different than this.

Of course, if this did prove true I still didn't see how it had anything to do with Veronica's murder. Still, it was worth checking out.

I paced across my office and sipped more coffee—just for the brain boost, of course—and it hit me that if Patrick really intended to divorce Veronica he wouldn't likely use Pike Warner, the firm that had represented his family for generations. No doubt he'd want to keep his plans under wraps until he was ready to confront Veronica.

Sure, the Pike Warner attorneys were supposed to uphold client confidentiality, but let's face it, things were leaked all the time, especially where millions of dollars—like in the Spencer-Taft estate—were at stake.

I needed some inside info. Usually I'd ask Jack to call his contact at Pike Warner and access the database that kept track of all lawsuits filed in the state. I couldn't do that this time. No way did I want to possibly generate a leak or start a vicious rumor that could cause major problems for Patrick—especially if my hunch wasn't true.

But I knew who I could ask.

I grabbed my cell phone from my handbag—a chic Prada satchel—then accessed the message log on my office phone and got the number Liam had left when he'd called last week for an appointment.

Liam worked at Schrader, Vaughn, and Pickett, a huge firm as old and respected as Pike Warner. Patrick would likely go there if he was planning to divorce Veronica. If that wasn't the case, Liam could access to the lawsuit database. Either way he could tell me what, if anything, Patrick was up to.

My stomach started to feel kind of gooey as I stared out the window and listened to the phone ring. I wasn't sure if it was my this-might-be-a-major-clue feeling, or my this-is-a-hot-guy feeling.

Then I knew.

Liam's voice came on the line and my belly got gooier. My toes even curled.

"What do you have when a lawyer's buried up to his neck in sand?" he asked. "Not enough sand."

I giggled—jeez, I couldn't stop giggling when I talked to him.

I forced myself to calm down and tried for some small

talk.

"How's your day going?" I asked.

"I have two calls on hold, three people in front of my desk, and I'm late for a meeting," Liam said. "But I'm making them all wait so I can talk to you."

Wow, I hadn't expected that.

Okay, now I felt kind of crappy that he was being so sweet—and I'd just called him to try and get some information.

I desperately racked my brain to come up with some less selfish reason to explain my call, but couldn't—damn, my sugar and caffeine had let me down—so I went with the truth.

"I was wondering if you could help me out with a little information," I said. "I'm planning a Thanksgiving feast for Patrick Spencer-Taft."

"Your clients in Calabasas," Liam said.

He'd actually remembered I'd told him that?

I hadn't expected that, either.

"I was working with his wife on the preparations," I said.

"I heard what happened," he said.

"I wanted to find out if Patrick was a client at your firm," I said.

I tried to make it sound light and chatty, as if it somehow related to the Thanksgiving festivities I was planning.

"What do you call a lawyer who violates attorney-client privilege?" Liam asked. "Disbarred."

I guess I had that coming.

At least he didn't sound offended or insulted.

"How about dinner tonight?" he asked.

No way had I expected that.

"I'd like it," I said, then it popped into my head that I was scheduled for a shift at Holt's tonight.

Damn. I hate that job.

"No, wait, sorry," I said. "I can't."

He paused, as if waiting for me to give him a reason. But no way was I telling him about my crappy part-time sales clerk job.

"Another time?" he asked.

"Sure," I said.

"Great," he said. "Saturday?"

My stomach got gooey all over again. "I can do Saturday."

We ended the call. My heart was pounding and my thoughts were completely scattered.

Before I could stagger back to my desk and collapse, my cell phone rang. It was Andrea.

"Something weird is going on," she said. "You'd better get out here right away."

Chapter 12

Andrea must have been watching for me because just as I pulled into the driveway the front door opened and she stepped outside. I had no idea what weird thing she needed me to take care of, but she didn't look terribly upset or panicked.

I hoped that meant there hadn't been another murder.

"I got a call from Poppy," Andrea said, as I got out of my Honda. "She said all the plans for the feast had changed."

Okay, now I might murder someone.

"Then Sasha called saying the same thing," she went on. "The construction crew is here. I don't know whether to let them keep working or not. What's going on?"

"Nothing's changed," I said, and told her how Poppy and Sasha had come to my office with their last-minute ideas. "I'm sticking with the original plan, the one Veronica came up with. We're doing this event the way she wanted it done."

Andrea heaved a sigh. "Thank goodness."

"I'll go check on things," I said.

Andrea went back inside and I circled to the west side of the house where the feast would take place. The workmen were busy carrying out the plans we'd discussed for the dance floor, the bandstand, and the kids' area. The tables and chairs would be delivered and set up Thursday morning when the caterer and servers got there, along with the florist. I found Lyle, the foreman of the work crew L.A. Affairs often used, and did a walk-through. There were no problems. Everything was on schedule and would be finished in plenty of time for the feast.

I looped around to the rear of the house, expecting to see Brandie and some of the others in the pool or relaxing on the patio, but nobody was there. I hoped that meant they were out sightseeing, for Andrea's sake.

When I stepped through the sliding glass doors into the family room, I spotted Erika tapping on her iPad. She must have just arrived because I hadn't noticed her car in the driveway when I'd pulled up.

This was the first time I'd seen her since the day Veronica was murdered. I wondered what she was doing here. Had Patrick decided to continue with the renovations? Or was she here for another reason?

She glanced up. "Oh. Haley. Hello."

Erika looked magnificent, as always—perfect hair and makeup, impeccably dressed in a YSL business suit. I couldn't see one single thing wrong with her appearance— which was kind of annoying.

If we were in middle school I'd have started a rumor about her.

We weren't in middle school, of course—but I saw no reason not to start something.

"I'm surprised to see you here," I said. "I'd heard you were a suspect in Veronica's murder."

Okay, that was an outright lie. But I needed to find out what—if anything—was going on between her and Patrick, and I didn't want to waste a lot of time dancing around the subject.

"*What?*" Erika's eyes widened and her mouth fell open. "That's outrageous. I had nothing to do with

Veronica's death. Nothing. Absolutely nothing."

Her denial seemed a bit over the top to me. I wasn't sure whether to believe her or not.

"You were in the house when Veronica was pushed off the balcony," I said.

"I came inside with Julia," she told me.

Considering that I also suspected Julia, I didn't see this as an air-tight alibi.

"You didn't slip away?" I asked. "Go upstairs?"

"Of course not," Erika insisted. "Why would I kill Veronica?"

"So you could get Patrick back," I said.

Erika expression morphed from I'm-stunned into now-I-get-it.

"That's what this is all about?" she asked. "Patrick?"

"You can see where the police would think you did away with Veronica to get your old boyfriend back," I said.

Yeah, I know, I'd never actually heard the cops say that—but they might have. In fact, they probably had.

"Patrick lost his head," Erika said, as if that explained everything. "He married Veronica on a whim. She wasn't worthy of him. Everybody saw it. Just ask Julia, she'll agree."

I was sure Julia would agree. In fact, I figured it was she who'd recommended that Veronica hire Erika to decorate the house with the hope that putting her close to Patrick again might re-ignite their relationship.

"I had nothing to do with Veronica's death and I certainly wasn't angling to get Patrick back," Erika told me. "I suggest you talk to Julia. She indicated to me that there some sort of problem between Veronica and Patrick."

I wondered if that something was Patrick's plan to

divorce Veronica.

Or maybe it was Julia's plan to murder Veronica.

"If you'll excuse me." Erika put her nose in the air and left the room.

Regardless of Erika's denial, I couldn't dismiss her as a suspect. I couldn't dismiss Julia either.

Which of them had the most to gain by Veronica's death? I wondered. Erika could end up married to Patrick—with his millions and the prestige of the Spencer-Taft family name. Julia would have a suitable daughter-in-law.

Both were great motives for murder.

* * *

The crab-ass mood I'd successfully fought off for the last few days was back with a vengeance when I walked into Holt's for my shift.

I mean, really, can you blame me?

I could have been having dinner tonight with a hot lawyer, or hunting down a fabulous handbag, or buying myself that Louis Vuitton tote.

As soon as I clocked-in and saw my name listed under the accessories department on the schedule by the time clock, my spirits fell further. I was looking down the barrel of four hours of my life that I would never get back, straightening rows of socks and displays of panty hose, belts, and house-brand handbags.

I didn't know how things could get worse.

Then they did.

When I stepped onto the sales floor, I spotted Gerri. She was sizing blouses in the juniors department, taking each one off the rack, checking the tag, and re-hanging it behind the correct size divider.

Oh my God, was she really that concerned about doing a great job—or deciding which styles to steal on her next trip into the stockroom?

No way could I stand here and do nothing.

That's how I roll.

Maybe I couldn't figure out who murdered Veronica, but I could do something to stop an employee from stealing from Holt's.

I walked up to Gerri and said, "I need your help in the stockroom."

She nodded quickly. "Oh, sure. Of course."

I led the way down the crowded aisles and through the double doors near the customer service booth, then continued past the shelving units to the receiving area. As usual, nobody was back here. We had the place to ourselves.

I whipped around. She froze.

"I know you stole those panties," I told her. "I saw you. You're probably stealing from Wal-Mart, too. I saw you parked at the edge of their lot so you can make a quick getaway. I'm telling the store manager, and I'm calling Wal-Mart."

She burst out crying

Oh, crap.

This really took some of the fun out of the whole thing for me.

Gerri covered her face with her palms and sobbed. Tears rolled down her face. Her shoulders rose and fell with each ragged breath.

Okay, now I felt like a jerk.

I caught her elbow and led her to the bedding section. I pulled two Laura Ashley bed-in-a-bag sets off the shelf and we sat down.

I'm not good with a crier, so I waited until she wound down.

"You're right," Gerri finally managed to say, as she wiped her cheeks with the backs of her hands. "I stole those panties. I stole food from other employees' lunches, too."

Oh my God, I'd solved *two* crimes?

"But I never took anything from Wal-Mart. Never," she said. "That's not why I park over there."

"So what's going on?" I asked.

"I've been sleeping in my car," Gerri said.

Oh, crap. Now I really felt like a jerk.

"I had a roommate and we shared an apartment," she explained. "Only she stopped paying the rent and got us kicked out. I couldn't afford it on my own—I can't afford anything on my own. I'm trying to save enough money to find a place but it's all I can do to keep gas in my car and eat. I'm hoping that if I do a really good job here, they'll keep me on after Christmas."

"I'd noticed you kissing up to Rita," I said.

"I hate her."

"That makes you my new best friend," I said.

A little laugh bubbled up, bringing on a fresh wave of tears from Gerri. She gulped them down.

"I stay with some of my friends when I can," she said, "but I can't really expect anyone to let me live with them permanently when I can't contribute to the rent."

"What about your family?" I asked.

"It's just me and my mom," she said, and tears pooled in her eyes. "She's barely getting by and she's already helping with my school expenses. I can't ask her for anything else. I just need to get through the next few months. I only have one more semester left of college. I'm going to be a nurse."

"A nurse, huh?" I asked. "Wow."

"Then I can get a good job at a hospital and everything will be fine," Gerri said and managed a small smile. "You're not really going to tell the store manager what I did, are you? I won't take anything else. I promise. And I can pay the store back for the panties I took, once I start working."

She'd been put in a very difficult position but was working hard to hang in there and finish school, even if she'd made some mistakes along the way. I didn't see how ratting her out and getting her fired was going to correct those mistakes.

"As long as you promise not to steal anything else," I said.

"I won't," Gerri said, shaking her head. "I swear."

"Okay, then I won't say anything," I told her.

She heaved a big sigh. "You won't regret this. I promise."

We got up and re-shelved the Laura Ashley bed-in-a-bag sets.

"Everything is going to be fine. I just know it," Gerri said, as we headed toward the stockroom doors. "Next year at this time I'm going to have a great job making a lot of money, I'll have a new car, and I can go see my mom for Thanksgiving."

Oh, jeez. There was that Thanksgiving thing again.

Then it hit me what she'd said.

"You're not going home for Thanksgiving?" I asked.

"I volunteered to come in on Black Friday to help set up everything for the sales," she said. "Mom was disappointed—me too, of course—but she understood that

I had to work."

Somebody really wanted to spend Thanksgiving with their mom?

How weird was that?

As Gerri pushed through the swinging door ahead of me I felt my cell phone vibrate in my pocket. I yanked it out and—oh my God—Liam was calling. I fell back into the stockroom and answered.

"Why can't you find lawyers sunbathing on the beach?" he asked. "Cats keep covering them with sand."

I laughed—I couldn't help it.

"Are you a Federal agent working undercover as an event planner?" Liam asked.

I didn't know where that question had come from but it sure as heck made me sound cool.

"Yes, I am," I said.

"Good," he replied, sounding businesslike all of a sudden. "Because if you were operating in some sort of official capacity and you requested information on a client, I could help you out—under the right circumstances, of course."

Okay, this conversation had taken a weird turn.

"Let me give you an example," he said. "Let's say you called and asked about a specific client. Let's say you wanted to know if he was represented by the firm I work for."

Then it hit me—he was talking about my phone call to him earlier today.

"And let's say I discovered that person was, in fact, a client of my firm," Liam went on. "Understand?"'

Oh my God, this was some sort of lawyer-code-talking. It was so cool.

"So if that happened could you, for instance, tell me if

the client was seeking a divorce?" I asked.

Liam paused for a few seconds, then said, "Hypothetically, I could say this client was doing just the opposite."

Obviously, I'd been wrong about Patrick secretly trying to divorce Veronica—and I was glad.

"Can I see you before Saturday?" Liam asked.

The change in topics surprised me—and I was glad about that too.

"How about tonight?" he asked.

I was tempted—really tempted. But I still had several hours to work and no way did I want him seeing how bad I looked at the end of my shift.

"Tomorrow?" he asked. "No, not tomorrow. I can't do tomorrow. How about Thursday?"

"Thursday is Thanksgiving," I reminded him.

"You have the feast at noon," he said.

Wow, did he remember everything I ever said to him?

"I have to go to my mom's afterwards," I said.

Liam must have picked up on the total lack of enthusiasm in my voice for Thanksgiving with my family because he said, "Not looking forward to spending the afternoon at your mom's, huh?"

"Not exactly," I told him.

It was the nicest thing I could think of.

"Okay, I'll see you on Saturday," he said, and I was relieved he hadn't asked for details.

We ended the call and for a few seconds I just stood there with the phone still pressed to my ear, enjoying the afterglow of our conversation—something about Liam affected me that way.

I was grateful that he'd gotten me the info I'd asked for, and he'd done it in a way that hadn't violated his ethics. I liked that about him.

I was starting to like a lot of things about him.

Then something flew into my head.

Since Patrick wasn't planning to divorce Veronica, the announcement she intended to make couldn't have had anything to do with him—anything bad, that is.

So what was it?

And did it have something to do with her murder?

I didn't see how.

I really hoped Jack had come up with something on the blackmailer theory.

Chapter 13

It was a Fendi day. Definitely a Fendi day.

I dashed around my bedroom pulling together the accessories for my navy blue business suit, gathering the things I needed for today and dropping them into my Fendi handbag. I loved the bag and I hadn't carried it in a while. Still, it didn't make up for the I-know-it's-out-there-somewhere handbag of my dreams that I was destined to find.

With a final check of my hair and makeup, I left my apartment and went downstairs to my car. I was actually on time this morning—not bad for hump day—and considered swinging through the Starbucks drive-thru—I mean, really, it's not a big deal to be a few minutes late for work—when I spotted a black Land Rover parked next to my Honda.

No way would I be on time now—and I'd definitely need a Starbucks.

Jack got out of the Land Rover as I walked over. He was dressed in jeans, CAT boots, and a black T-shirt. He had a little beard going. I figured he'd been up all night, working.

Jeez, how come I never looked that hot after an all-nighter?

"What have you found out?" Jack asked.

It wasn't like him to be quite this intense, so I figured he was still under serious pressure to find out who'd murdered Veronica.

"Two suspects," I said, and told him my suspicions about Julia and Erika, then had to admit that I'd come up with only kind-of-sort-of motives and no evidence.

"I been running your blackmailer theory to ground," Jack said. "Bank records indicate Veronica had taken more money out of their account than usual, but nothing significant. Small amounts every few days for the last several weeks."

"She could have been spending it on herself, or on the new house," I said.

"Or by withdrawing small amounts frequently, she might have figured she wouldn't arouse suspicion," Jack said.

The blackmail theory made more sense than my suspicion of Julia and Erika—especially in view of the fact that Patrick had told me that he and Veronica had had several conversations about how much money she was spending lately.

"That would mean she probably met with the blackmailer often," Jack said.

A vision popped into my head that made me shiver. I pushed it out.

"But if she was cooperating, why would he—or she— kill her?" I asked.

"Maybe she got tired of being the goose that had to keep laying the golden eggs," Jack said, "and threatened to go to the police."

"Do you think whoever it was came to the house, confronted her, then killed her to keep her quiet?" I asked.

"Security in that neighborhood amounts to getting past the gate guard. It wouldn't be a problem for someone determined to gain access," Jack said. "There was a lot of commotion at the house. Workers coming and going. Lots of different faces. One more in the crowd wouldn't draw attention."

We were quiet for a moment, then Jack said, "I want to get this case wrapped up before the Thanksgiving feast tomorrow. The house will be full of the candy company employees, plus the event support staff."

"Will you be there?" I asked.

He nodded. "I'll have a team in place."

There had been no threats to the Spencer-Taft family or any indication that something terrible might happen, but it was Jack's job to be more safe than sorry.

"I'll keep digging," I said.

Jack nodded, then walked with me to my car. I clicked the lock and he opened the door for me. I squeezed past him. Wow, he smelled great—even after being up all night. He stepped back. I gave him a quick wave as I drove away.

Okay, now I was really late. Still, I had to take care of the errands that I'd planned to handle this morning.

I drove to Holt's—it was only a few minutes from my apartment—and pulled into the parking lot at the rear of the building. The store wasn't open yet, but things were hopping. A big-rig was backed into the loading dock and the truck team was hustling to empty it. A garbage truck lumbered toward the Dumpster. About a dozen cars were parked nearby and employees were heading inside.

I slid into a spot, then hurried up the steps beside the loading dock and into the stockroom.

A weird little voice in my head had been bugging me since I talked with Gerri. I'd promised her I wouldn't rat her out to Jeanette, the store manager, about what she'd done, but I couldn't just let it go.

I hurried through the stockroom, pushed open the swinging doors into the store, and went to Jeanette's office.

* * *

As I got out of the elevator and headed down the hallway toward L.A. Affairs, my cell phone rang. I dug it out of my handbag and saw that Mom was calling.

I was hardly in the mood to deal with her so early in the morning—I hadn't even had coffee yet and that whole thing with Gerri was still bouncing around my head—but I figured it was better to get it over with now and be clear for the rest of the day.

"Good news," Mom said, when I answered. "I've found the most charming young man for your sister."

I wondered if it was the Cuban guy she'd mentioned earlier.

"This has been quite the search," Mom said. "I know they're going to hit it off splendidly."

I wasn't convinced either of the parties involved would agree, but I didn't bother to say so.

"Sounds good, Mom," I said.

Really, what else could I say?

"I'll see you tomorrow," Mom said and ended the call.

I paused outside the entrance to L.A. Affairs to drop my phone into my handbag, and it rang again. Mom was calling back already? But when I checked the ID screen I saw Andrea's name.

"You need to get out here," she said, when I answered.

Oh my God, she sounded like she was in total panic mode.

"Brandie is missing," she said. "I can't find her

anywhere."

Okay, now I was in total panic mode.

"I've looked everywhere I can think to look," Andrea told me. "I've called her cell phone over and over. I texted her. She hasn't responded to anything."

"Did you call the private security team?" I asked, already heading toward the elevator.

"They're searching the grounds," Andrea said. "You ... you don't think she was kidnapped, do you?"

If Veronica was actually being blackmailed, it was possible, now that she was gone, the blackmailer had ramped up to kidnapping. Jack had said the family might be targeted in some way.

"I mean, where would she go? How would she get anywhere?" Andrea said. "I called the gate guard. No taxis came through this morning. The limo service hasn't been here."

"Her mom and aunts must be going crazy," I said.

"They're still sleeping," Andrea said. "Should I wake them? I mean, I'm not sure. I don't want to alarm them, if it's nothing."

"The security team will know what to do. Just sit tight. I'm on my way," I said, and ended the call.

I punched the elevator call button, trying to still my runaway thoughts. Really scary images bloomed in my mind. I forced them out and concentrated on the situation.

Maybe Brandie had just gone for a walk. Maybe she'd found a secluded spot and hunkered down to text her friends back home. Maybe she had her ear buds in and hadn't heard Andrea calling for her. Maybe she was being a typical teenager and wasn't in the mood to answer her phone.

All those things were possible, but not likely.

The elevator doors opened and I rushed inside.

Maybe she'd really been kidnapped.

What else could it be? Andrea had a point. Brandie had no way of getting anywhere, and even if she'd found a way, there were few places open at this time of day. So what other alternative was there?

Then it hit me.

I knew exactly where Brandie was and how she'd gotten there.

* * *

"How'd you find me?" Brandie asked.

I held up my cell phone. "The Starbucks app. I get a message every time it's used."

I'd checked it as soon as I'd stepped into the elevator and seen exactly where Brandie was, then called Jack and told him where I was headed. When I'd driven into the shopping center and spotted Brandie seated at an umbrella table outside Starbucks sipping a frappuccino, I'd texted Andrea and Jack with the news.

I nodded toward Veronica's white BMW parked nearby.

"Told you I could drive," Brandie said.

The trip from the house to Starbucks was through quiet residential streets, so it wasn't like she was navigating the freeway during the morning commute. That didn't make it right—but it wasn't my place to say so. Her mom could handle that conversation.

"I need coffee," I said.

The line was short so I got my drink quickly, loaded it up with sugar and creamer, and joined Brandie at the table outside.

She had a little sullen-belligerent-I-don't-care-what-anybody-thinks teenage attitude going so I sipped my drink and let a few minutes pass before I said anything.

"Everybody thought you'd been kidnapped," I told her.

She looked at me as if I'd lost my mind and said, "Are you kidding me?"

"After what happened to Veronica," I said, "the security team is thinking worst-case-scenario."

She pouted for a moment, then gasped. "Oh my God, does my mom know about this? She always sleeps late. I figured I'd be back before she woke up."

"She doesn't know yet," I said.

Brandie slumped in her chair. "This vacation is so lame. Veronica was always really cool, and now she's not here anymore. Mom and my aunts are always fighting. That tour guide keeps sending us to stupid places."

I couldn't disagree. This hadn't exactly been a dream vacation.

"Everybody said I could come out here for college, but Patrick won't want me here now," Brandie said. "He won't pay for my classes. I know he won't. He wouldn't even give my uncle a decent job. He made him a gardener. I'm not going to clean the house or something, just to go to college here."

A few seconds passed—I mean, jeez, I was drinking my coffee—until I realized what she'd said.

"Your uncle?" I asked. "What uncle?"

"Darrell," she said. "He's, you know, that relative nobody wants to talk about, sort of like Veronica's mother. I didn't even know he'd come out here."

"Did he contact you?" I asked.

Brandie sipped her frappie and shook her head. "I saw him. At the house. The day we arrived."

I remembered that while her mom and aunts were piling out of the limo and gawking at the house, Brandie had been looking at the workmen.

"I guess he was kind of embarrassed about us seeing him working as a gardener," Brandie said, "because as soon as he saw me, he took off."

Oh my God, a relative of Veronica's had been at the house the day she was murdered? Working with the gardeners? And he'd taken off when Brandie recognized him?

"I'll be right back," I said.

I hopped out of my chair and paced a few feet away as I called Jack on my cell phone. He answered right away.

"I think I found Veronica's blackmailer," I told him.

Chapter 14

"That really hot guy is here looking for you," Bella said.

I was crouched down in front of the wall of jeans in the juniors department, checking my cell phone. It was the perfect spot to avoid being seen by one of the store's managers—and customers, of course—but, luckily, Bella knew where to find me.

I sprang to my feet and shoved my cell phone into my pocket. I didn't know which hot guy Bella was referring to—not that there're a lot of them dropping in on me at Holt's—but I hoped it was Jack or Shuman.

"Where?" I asked, craning my neck to see around the customers swarming through the aisles.

Honestly, I didn't know why so many people were in the store tonight. The Stuff-It sale, apparently, was too much of an allure to keep folks at home preparing for Thanksgiving tomorrow.

I'd spent most of the day getting my clients' holiday parties finished. After Jack had showed up at Starbucks and we'd made a plan, I'd called Detective Shuman, who'd contacted the homicide detectives investigating Veronica's murder. Between confirming florists and caterers, handling a few last minute changes, and finding a bakery who'd take a twelve dozen cupcakes rush order, I'd learned that Darrell had been picked up and was being questioned by the police.

I spotted Jack standing near the customer service booth and my heart lurched—for a couple of reasons.

"Ask him if he has a brother," Bella called as I walked away.

Jack looked tired and a bit grim—and still really hot, of course—as I walked past him. He followed me through the swinging doors into the stockroom.

"Darrell admitted to taking money from Veronica," Jack said. "Claims he wasn't blackmailing her. He just wanted what was due him."

Money from Pammy Candy, no doubt.

"I think he's lying," Jack said. "So do the cops."

I figured Jack had a contact in the police department who'd been sending him info. Jack had contacts everywhere.

"Why else would Darrell have gotten a job with the landscapers so he could get near her?" I asked. "What about Veronica's death? Has he admitted to killing her?"

Jack shook his head. "He says he had nothing to do with it."

"So it's just a coincidence that Darrell was at the house the morning she was murdered?" I asked. "I don't believe it."

"Nobody believes it," Jack agreed. "The cops will keep up the pressure. He'll confess."

I relaxed knowing Darrell was in custody and the case would be wrapped up soon. Jack seemed relieved, too. I could only imagine how Patrick and the rest of the family felt.

"Are you keeping the security team in place at the house for the feast tomorrow?" I asked.

"They'll be security present, but I'll cut back," Jack said, "so my team can spend the day with their families."

"What about you?" I asked.

He hesitated a moment, then said, "I'll be on scene."

Jack had never been forthcoming about his family. In fact, last Thanksgiving we'd ended up working a case together. I decided not to pry.

"I'll be there early to make sure everything is prepped and ready to go when the guests arrive," I said.

He gave me a little grin—Jack has a killer grin—then left.

Honestly, I felt a million times better knowing Darrell was in custody. Even though I'd been totally wrong about suspecting Julia and Erika of Veronica's murder, I was okay with it. All that mattered was that Darrell would confess, the case would be closed, everybody could enjoy the feast tomorrow, and I didn't have to worry about something bad happening—until I got to Mom's house, of course.

As I walked out of the stockroom I spotted Gerri straightening racks of pants in the misses department. She saw me in the same instant.

"Haley, you're not going to believe what happened," she said, and hurried over. "The store manager called me into her office as soon as I got here this afternoon."

Oh, crap.

I wasn't expecting to be confronted by Gerri.

"She told me there's a Holt's scholarship for nursing students," Gerri said, and a big smile bloomed on her face. "She gave me almost three thousand dollars."

I just smiled.

"Three thousand dollars. That's so much money," Gerri said. "Now I can get a place to live. And she told me I can work more hours—all I want. I can even stay on after Christmas. Isn't that awesome?"

"Great news," I said.

Gerri gasped. "Oh, and the best part is that she gave me the day off tomorrow—with pay. Now I can go home for Thanksgiving."

"That's wonderful," I said, because, really, it was.

Her eyes got big and she heaved a huge sigh.

"Three thousand dollars—that's a ton of money," she said. "Do you know what you can do with three thousand dollars?"

I knew you could buy a Louis Vuitton tote bag with it. Or not.

* * *

"Oh, Haley, honey, I could just cry," Melanie said.

Usually, I'm not good with a crier—but I thought I could handle it this time.

Honestly, I didn't blame her.

We were on the west lawn of the Spencer-Taft home and I was giving her a preview of the festivities that would begin in a few hours when the Pammy Candy employees arrived for the feast. I'd been here all morning making sure everything would be in place.

It was a typical Southern California day—sunny, mild, and gorgeous. We might not have forests of trees boasting fall-colored leaves, but we made up for it with our weather.

The florist and her staff were turning the grounds into a harvest showplace with bales of hay, corn stalks, pumpkins and gourds, and mum plants. Servers were setting the tables in the dining area with brown linens, accented with amber, garnet, and hunter green floral arrangements. Two workmen were fixing a minor problem with the lighting.

"This section is for the kids," I said, as we strolled along.

A maze had been created with hay bales. There was a kid-sized table with building blocks and another for crafts.

"There will be face-painting," I said, "and games like relay and three-legged races. All the staff will be in pilgrim costumes."

Melanie dabbed the corner of her eyes and said, "Veronica would have loved this."

"These are her ideas," I said. "Everything."

"You've done a wonderful job bringing her vision to life," Melanie said. "Truly you have."

We walked past the bandstand and the dance floor, and circled back toward the house.

"Well, this trip didn't turn out like we thought it would," Melanie said. "We're leaving tomorrow, you know."

With everything that had been going on in the past few days, I hadn't learned about their plans to leave. I hadn't heard, either, whether Melanie knew of Brandie's excursion to Starbucks. I sure as heck hadn't told her.

"The funeral will be on Monday," Melanie said. "I think Patrick wanted to bury her out here, but his mother convinced him it was best to take her back home and lay her to rest with her family."

I hadn't seen Patrick yet today but I wasn't surprised. Getting through the feast, no doubt thinking of Veronica every moment, would be tough.

"Thank goodness there's a suspect in custody," Melanie said.

Apparently, she didn't know the suspect was a member of her own family.

I wasn't going to tell her that, either.

"And Pammy Candy will keep turning out delicious treats," Melanie said, and managed a smile. "Veronica would be just pleased as punch about that."

My cell phone rang. Melanie gave me a quick wave and went into the house as I glanced at the screen and saw that Jack was calling.

"How's it going?" he asked.

From the background noise, I figured he was driving.

"No problems," I said.

"I've got two men in place," Jack said. "I'll be there in a few minutes."

I'd seen his men dressed in suits, standing like sentinels watching over the grounds.

"Anything new on Darrell?" I asked.

"Nothing yet," Jack said.

I'd hoped Darrell would have confessed by now. From the tone of Jack's voice, I knew he'd wished for the same.

"See you in a few," he said, and we ended the call.

I went into the house through the west entrance and walked down the hallway past the bathroom and the den, then turned into the massive kitchen. The caterer had been here for hours and the place smelled delicious. Cooks were busy tending the two stoves, the double ovens, and chopping veggies at the worktable.

The menu was extensive—turkey, ham, beef, fish, plus all the traditional side dishes. I'd seen the selection of pies they'd brought in for dessert—so yummy looking I wanted to lay my face down in one and eat my way to the tin.

Julia walked in. She stopped short just inside the doorway when she saw me. I was surprised to see her, too.

She looked exquisite, of course, magnificently turned out in a conservative skirt and blazer that screamed I'm-here-under-protest.

"I'm assuming the hostessing duties today," she said. "It was called for, under the circumstances."

I figured she would have shoved Erika into the position alongside Patrick, had it not been the height of bad taste.

Julia nodded oh-so-slightly toward the large windows that overlooked the grounds.

"The job you've done is most favorable," she said in her always careful, measured tone. "I'll have my assistant call L.A. Affairs on Monday with my compliments."

As if she were doing me a favor.

I liked her less and less every time I saw her.

"The ideas were all Veronica's," I told her. "She approved all the plans."

Julia uttered a laugh. "If you say so."

She kept gazing out the window and finally said, "Thank goodness this ordeal is almost over."

Then I felt kind of bad. Julia—along with everyone else in the family—had been through an emotional trauma these past few days. Maybe I should cut her some slack.

"They're leaving tomorrow," Julia said.

She'd said it in an off-handed way, as if she was merely thinking aloud. It struck me as odd.

"There's still the funeral," I pointed out.

Julia turned to me and shrugged. "The family will have a presence there, of course."

Beyond her through the window, I spotted Jack walking onto the grounds. He was dressed in a dark suit. I wondered if he had a gun in a shoulder holster under the jacket.

"Patrick's father will meet him there," Julia went on. "Our attorney will be on hand in case there's any … unpleasantness regarding that company."

"You mean Pammy Candy?" I asked.

She shuddered. "Really, could that girl have picked a more common, tasteless name for a business?" she asked.

"It was a family name," I reminded her.

"Oh, yes, that family. Entrepreneurs, all of them," Julia lifted her chin. "Fanny packs. Seasonal fanny packs, at that. They honestly thought my Patrick would agree to put our name—our good family name—on such a horrible product. Ridiculous."

Through the window I saw Jack stop and speak to one of the security guys, then disappear from view.

I was frantically formulating a good excuse to get away from Julia and go hang out with Jack when it hit me what she'd just said.

"You knew about Renee's idea for the fanny pack business?" I asked.

I couldn't imagine that Renée and Julia had spoken prior to their arrival at the house last week. So how had Julia learned about it?

"Did Veronica tell you?" I asked.

"Oh, yes. Another big idea she and that family of hers had come up with," Julia declared. She pressed her lips together. "I knew when I saw those people get out of the limousine wearing those things that something was going on. And, of course, Veronica admitted it as soon as I confronted her. She was actually proud of it."

Oh my God. There was only one place and one moment when they could have had that conversation.

"So you went upstairs and discussed it with Veronica as soon as her family arrived?" I asked.

"I certainly did," Julia told me.

Behind her in the kitchen doorway, Jack appeared.

"I was not going to stand in front of this house and welcome them, as if I were hostessing," Julia told me. "I went inside. Erika had the good sense to come, too. I asked her to go to the kitchen and alert the cooks while I went upstairs to find Veronica. Really, to have guests—even guests of that nature—and not be present upon their arrival. It's simply not done. I intended to tell her that."

I got a yucky feeling.

"Veronica didn't know that?" I asked.

"She knew nothing," Julia said, agitated now. "I should have realized sooner that something was amiss with Patrick. He kept delaying his return from back east. I never thought that some small town, average girl was keeping him there. I should have stepped in sooner. I should have never allowed his father to send him there in the first place."

The noise level in the kitchen dropped. The caterer's staff had turned to us. Julia, caught up in memories and growing more upset by the minute, didn't seem to notice.

"You went upstairs to the master bedroom suite," I said. "You saw Veronica there, and she told you about the fanny pack business."

"She bragged about it," Julia said, her voice rising slightly. "And then—then—she thought she could actually calm my horror at the news by informing me of an announcement she intended to make. As if I should feel special that she'd told me before anyone else."

I yucky feeling got yuckier.

"They intended to start a family next year," Julia said, her eyes blazing. "I would never have gotten rid of her, if that had happened."

Yeah, I was feeling totally yucky now.

"She had no idea I'd become upset. She actually thought I'd be pleased. Can you imagine?" Julia said. "She ran out onto the balcony. I followed her. She began

to scream like the scattered-brain girl that she was, and I—
"

Julia froze. She glanced around the room and saw that the caterer's staff was staring.

"So you pushed her?" I asked softly.

"Of course not. Don't be ridiculous," she told me. "Now, if you'll excuse me."

Julia turned to leave but stopped short at the sight of Jack blocking the doorway. No way could she get around him.

She turned to me again and drew herself up. "You think you've discovered something? That I've confessed to something?"

I didn't say anything.

Julia uttered a bitter laugh. "People like me don't get convicted."

"Mrs. Spencer-Taft," Jack said softly, "would you come with me, please? We need to call your attorney."

He stepped back and gestured down the hallway. Julia put her nose in the air and walked out of the kitchen.

Jack followed her.

Chapter 15

I left.

I made sure everything was set for the feast, told Andrea and all the vendors to call me if a problem arose, then said goodbye to Melanie, Cassie, Renée, and Brandie, and left.

Julia was sequestered with a team of attorneys. Jack was locked away with another team of attorneys. The homicide detectives had been called. Patrick hadn't shown up yet.

No way did I want to be there when he arrived.

Going to Mom's for Thanksgiving sounded better than staying at the Spencer-Taft home—that's how bad I didn't want to be there—even if I'd likely end up listening to a history lesson about Cuba through dinner.

I pulled out of the driveway and drove away without a backward look. The streets were quiet. Everyone was inside eating turkey, I figured.

Darrell was off the hook—for murder, anyway. I guessed we'd never know for sure if he was blackmailing Veronica to keep quiet about her mom being in prison, or if she was willingly giving him money.

It was small consolation to know that I'd been right all along about Veronica's planned announcement leading to her death. Hearing that she and Patrick intended to start a family in the coming year had, apparently, been the final straw for Julia.

At the corner I stopped while two catering vans drove past. Seemed nobody in Calabasas was cooking for themselves today.

I turned right, thinking that I might have figured everything out sooner if Patrick had told me what the big announcement was. I guess he'd been too busy running Pammy Candy to realize how important it was to Veronica, and that she'd planned to make a big deal out of it.

Then, too, I might have realized Julia was the murderer if I'd known she'd been lying right from the start. She'd probably figured the police would eventually determine that Veronica was pushed from the balcony so she'd muddied the waters with the story of Veronica leaving Patrick, moving back home, and committing suicide.

Whether Julia would ever get what was coming to her, I didn't know. She had an excellent team of lawyers and millions of dollars.

I wasn't sure her freedom would mean much, since her son would likely never speak to her again.

I turned another corner and rolled up to the security gate. The guard was on duty, checking I.D.s, waving people in. The gate slid open and, as I drove through, I noticed a car parked at the curb. A man was standing next to it.

Oh my God. It was Liam.

He was dressed in khaki pants and a pale blue shirt. The breeze had ruffled his hair. He straightened away from the fender when he saw me and shot me a big smile.

I pulled up behind his car. He opened the door for me and I got out.

"What do you call a lawyer who shows up with a picnic lunch on Thanksgiving?" he asked. "A potential boyfriend."

My insides got all gooey.

I looked inside his car and saw a big wicker picnic basket and a blanket on the back seat. I was totally impressed—with his initiative and the effort he'd put into finding me today.

"Have you been waiting long?" I asked.

"All my life," he said, and grinned.

Now my toes were curling, too.

"I got the idea you'd be okay with showing up late to your mom's house," he said.

"Mom who?" I said, and he chuckled.

"I know a great spot not far from here," Liam said. "How about it?"

"Sure," I said.

"I'll drive." He told the guard we were leaving my car parked there for a while, then we both got in his car and he drove us to a park a couple of miles away.

We had the place to ourselves, as he spread out the blanket under a tree and unpacked the picnic basket. There were big, hearty turkey sandwiches, potato salad, chocolate-chip cookies, and two bottles of wine.

"What do you call a lawyer who tries to get a girl drunk on the first date?" he asked. "Thinking ahead."

He passed me a plate loaded with food, and a glass of wine. We ate and chatted for a while.

"Can I get your opinion on something?" he asked.

I was feeling pretty mellow—though I wasn't sure if it was from the wine or Liam's presence.

He pulled his cell phone from his pocket and started scrolling through screens.

"My sister works at Neiman Marcus. They just got these in stock and they're holding them for a mid-

December sale," he said. "But she thought my other sister would love one so she suggested I buy it for her for Christmas. What do you think?"

Liam passed me his cell phone and—oh my God—there was the most fabulous handbag I'd ever seen. My heart started to beat faster. It was a gorgeous clutch in rich dark leather with a ruby Swarovski crystal clasp.

"I love this bag." I might have said that kind of loud.

Liam leaned back a little.

"I absolutely must have it." Yeah, I really said that too loud. I offered him a quick smile. "I'm kind of a nut about designer handbags."

"To designer handbags," he said, and lifted his wine glass. We toasted and drank, then he said. "I can ask my sister to hold one for you."

"I need two," I said. "One for my best friend Marcie."

"No problem," he said.

Oh my God, this was my best Thanksgiving ever.

Then something hit me.

"Hey, wait," I said. "Aren't you supposed to spend Thanksgiving with your family?"

"Mom had us going to dinner at the house of a friend of hers," Liam said. "Some place out in La Cañada Flintridge."

Wow, that was a coincidence. My mom and dad lived in La Cañada Flintridge.

"Mom had been friends with this woman for years," Liam said. "Don't laugh, but my mom used to be in beauty pageants."

Okay, that was weird. My mom used to be in beauty pageants.

"There was some talk about a daughter who was a model," he said.

Huh. My sister did some modeling.

"I think it was a set up," he said

I got a weird feeling.

Liam shook his head. "It didn't sound like a great idea to me—the setup or the dinner."

My weird feeling got totally weird.

"She was serving Cuban food," he said. "Crazy, huh?"

Oh my God—*oh my God*.

Liam was the guy. The one Mom had picked out for my sister.

Oh, crap.

THE END

Dear Reader,

There's more Haley out there! If you enjoyed this novella, check out the other books in the series. They're available in hardcover, paperback, and ebook editions.

Looking for even more mystery? Meet Dana Mackenzie, my newest amateur sleuth, in Fatal Debt and Fatal Luck. Both are available in paperback and ebook editions.

I also write historical romance novels under the pen name Judith Stacy. Check them out at www.JudithStacy.com.

More information is available at www.DorothyHowellNovels.com., where there's always a giveaway going on! Join my Dorothy Howell Novels Facebook page, sign up for my newsletter, and follow me on twitter @DHowellNovels.

Thanks for adding my books to your library and recommending me to your friends and family.

Happy reading!
Dorothy

CPSIA information can be obtained
at www.ICGtesting.com
Printed in the USA
LVOW04s1504030816

498915LV00019B/1192/P

9 780985 693046